DARK TOYS AND
CONSUMER GOODS

DARK TOYS AND CONSUMER GOODS

Tales of a consumer society

Laurence Staig

For Mane
Jan best

![signature]

M
MACMILLAN CHILDREN'S BOOKS

First published in the United Kingdom 1989 by
MACMILLAN CHILDREN'S BOOKS
A division of Macmillan Publishers Limited
London and Basingstoke
Associated companies throughout the world

Paperback edition published 1990

British Library Cataloguing in Publication Data

Staig, Laurence
    Dark toys and consumer goods
    1. Children's short stories in English.
    1945 — Anthologies
    823'.01'089282J

ISBN 0-333-47562-3

Typeset by Matrix
21 Russell St, London WC2

Printed in Hong Kong

Acknowledgements

I'd like to thank the following for listening, advising and offering encouragement on many of the *Dark Toys* stories: Harriet MacDougal, Christine Willison, Mick Gowar, Ruth Craft, Barbara Machin, Jan Mark, Ramsey Campbell and Sharon Phipp; and the kids of South Carolina's high schools, class of '86, for giving me feedback.

Finally, special thanks to Lynnet Wilson of Macmillan.

With thanks, to Ray Bradbury

Contents

'Money makes the world go around.'

Cabaret

'He who Dies with the Most Toys, Wins.'

Message on an American T-shirt

Closed Circuit

Their mother had always been afraid of multi-storey car parks.

There was no particular reason for this, no easily identifiable explanation. She just was.

Something about mazes? Perhaps.

Now she would have to learn to love them.

The Anderson family had been awarded one of the remaining places in the Township. Happy Sterling was to be their new home. It had taken her husband years to accrue enough Government Credits to qualify for a Development Corporation place. She had even surrendered her own right to Employment Credits in order to hurry things along. The Ministry of Placing offered an entire range of incentives.

At last they were there, everything to hand and with no need to worry about disruptive minority groups such as the Rioters and the Campaigners. Just spoiling it for others. Besides, it seemed such a nice place to live.

She would have to try to live with the car park. There was nowhere else to shop and a car was the safest way to get around. In any case, Consumer Comfort Shopping Mall boasted that they could provide everything you would ever want, all under one roof.

It was an oppressive kind of day. The sky lay like a dirty grey blanket, threatening to flop down upon them at any moment. There had been a thickening of Meltdown Jetsam lately and that always played havoc with the weather, or so she had been told by a guard on the freeway. It would almost certainly rain, which could be the only good reason for getting 'under cover'.

Mrs Anderson took a deep breath and approached the ramp which led from Housing Zone Zero 9 to the Mall. The entrance peeped out from below a dark monolithic block of concrete. Windowless, it squatted, waiting, at the far end of the access lane.

At first they thought they were driving into an enormous silver fishing net. Only when the bonnet of the car was almost touching the gleaming chrome of the mesh did they realise that it was a portcullis.

They had reached the ticket dispenser. The car window wound slowly down. A small plastic card slid from the yellow meter as if it were offering its tongue for inspection.

Mrs Anderson took the card.

A synthesised voice crooned, 'Welcome to Happy Sterling, have a happy shopping trip,' and a green light flashed through the chrome mesh. Overhead, angry clouds shifted uneasily, globules of burn-out floated through the ozone as a spatter of raindrops hit the windscreen.

2

After a few moments the car advanced beneath the rising gate. Cautiously it crept into a dimly lit concrete cavern of invisible corridors and brief instructions:

UP, DOWN, LEFT, RIGHT, NO ENTRY, STAIRCASE, LEVEL 8

John had been silent until now.

A brilliantly lit sign flashed a reassuring message as they manoeuvred into the UP, LEVEL 8 Lane: 'No vandalism here thanks to CONSUMER COMFORT SHOPPING CIRCUIT Ltd.' Below these, there was a friendlier message in red:

'YOUR PEACE OF MIND IS OUR PEACE OF MIND.'

'How can they stop vandalism?' asked John.

His mother had also noticed the sign.

'Did you see what we had to get through to get in here!'

'Oh.'

To the left a further sign announced: 'You have entered at Level 8.'

The car park appeared to be almost full. It was vast and impersonal. Even cars which seemed to have their own character and appeal became cold and purely functional once they sat in a multi-storey.

Perhaps it was this that made her afraid.

The building was deserted except for the rows of vehicles, neatly positioned in their bays. There was an equal assortment of new and old cars, all shapes and sizes. John was prompted into considering the possible re-introduction of his car cleaning service.

There seemed to be a lot of cars in Happy Sterling. When they lived in the north he had supplemented his weekly pocket money by this little weekend enterprise. Only when they introduced the Class Zoning system did the bookings start to fall. Manchester and Liverpool had been classified as Resting Only sectors. His father had accrued enough Merits to be awarded a job, which meant they had to move south, along with everybody else who had earned that privileged status.

It seemed a good system to John, the Riot Class could all be kept together, out of the way of socially useful groups such as the Producers and the Investment City areas. Still, he was glad that he hadn't been born into an Investors' family group. He would have had to live in an Investors' sector like his phone-friend, Jimmy. They all wore special uniforms and always spoke 'Computer'. At least as a re-classified Consumer Class family the Andersons could wear what they liked. The area was noted for its islands of industry. Living standards here were really high. The Andersons were lucky. The Great Meltdown had given everyone the chance to start again, right from scratch.

John decided that the return of the 'Anderson Car Cleaning Service' was a must. Many of the cars seemed very dirty, almost abandoned. He decided that the township must be full of either very lazy or very busy people.

'This is crazy!' said his mother suddenly.

John had been so preoccupied with the various

4

models that he had not noticed their arrival at Level 1, the very top. John thought this a strange place to start numbering, surely you started at the bottom?

'Stay calm,' whispered Mrs Anderson, 'it'll make sense soon.'

She took a deep breath and drove on.

Julie, John's little sister, had been asleep in the back seat. With a yawn she sat up and looked through the rear window. They had left the north very early that morning and Julie always slept a lot.

'Are we there, Mummy?'

Mrs Anderson searched the level. She looked desperately for a space, or even the tell-tale indicators of a departing car. There was nothing.

The outside wind howled through the air vents and echoed across the gallery, the only indication of the storm. Rows upon rows of silent cars waited, patiently.

This was the largest multi-storey car park they had ever seen.

'Can we get out and see where we are?' asked Julie. 'Can we see our new house?'

'Don't be stupid!' snapped John. 'This is an enclosed car park, there's nothing to see. Anyway there wouldn't be anything to look at. Our estate's access-way goes straight into the Mall, it overlaps, stupid.'

Julie tried to picture this in her head, but gave up.

'Quiet, you kids,' said their mother.

Her nerves tingled.

'The centre must be packed but we've at least got

to get something to eat. Dad will be here tonight. The Development Corporation won't be delivering the packing cases till tomorrow. I guess it's down we go again.'

'Aren't there any other shops?' groaned John. 'I only want a hamburger.'

'Not according to their little blue handbook,' she replied.

They kept going down.

'CONSUMER COMFORT is the only place to shop as far as I can tell. Give me a break, John, we've only just moved here. I don't know the neighbourhood yet.'

John threw himself back in his seat. He was bored. He thought of all those cars again and mentally tried to calculate how much he could make if he got the job of cleaning all the cars on one level.

Slowly, their old estate car crept back down through the levels. Large yellow arrows directed them into narrow lanes. These, in turn, sub-divided into UP or DOWN or HALT. The options were clear.

LEVEL 7

LEVEL 8

The car crawled around a sharp hairpin bend and stopped.

'John?' Mrs Anderson squinted through the windscreen. 'Is it my imagination or what? I don't think I've seen one car leave since we got in here . . .' Her words faded and slowed.

For the first time she looked about her, taking

6

in the setting and layout of the car park. Cautiously she lowered the window and listened. They could hear nothing except the chug of the car 'tickover' and the polite rush of the air exchange system.

A sign on a nearby pillar indicated a direction:

EXIT TO LEVEL 8: BANKS AND FINANCE COMPLEX, GOODS DEPOSIT STATION (GROUND FLOOR ONLY).

She followed the direction of the arrow. It pointed to a large pair of port-holed swing doors. With a sharp command to the children to stay in the car, Mrs Anderson jumped out.

She crossed the vehicle lane towards the doors. Suddenly, she stopped. Through the stare of the double O were queues of people waiting at lifts. A corridor to the left was filled with a blur of figures pushing shopping trolleys. She laughed at herself for being so silly.

Of course there were other people here.

She skipped back to the car and got in.

'What is it, Mummy?' asked Julie.

'Nothing sweetheart, Mummy had a peculiar thought, that's all. It's going to be crowded. All our new neighbours must be doing their shopping today.'

She reached into the glove compartment. There were still some chewing tablets there. John shared them out.

A voice in her head told her to stay strong. If you're a Consumer Class citizen you take the rough with the smooth. She would have to get tougher.

They drove down another ramp.

Again Mrs Anderson brought the car to a halt.
She counted in her head.

LEVEL 8, that was where they had started, ground
level. The Consumer Comfort Mall was a twelve-level
shopping centre according to the corporation guide
book. But four levels underground?

'Mum!' whined John.

With a low whistle at the thought of 'underground
cities' she shrugged her shoulders, engaged gear and
moved off.

LEVEL 9

LEVEL 10.

This level was darker than the others, many of
the lights did not seem to work. A wall had been
re-treated, a shadow of letters showed that graffiti
had been daubed on it at some time.

She chewed harder.

LEVEL 11

LEVEL 12.

The last floor. There was space.

With an enormous sigh of relief Mrs Anderson
manoeuvred the car into one of the bays and
switched off the ignition. She had not noticed how
wet her hands were. She whispered a sentence of
self-congratulation. To get round a multi-storey was
one thing but to run through twelve floors and end
up parked underground was another.

They had parked next to a gleaming 1999 Westland

Coupé. John jumped out first and rushed over. His fingers rested lightly on the paintwork and then admiringly stroked the highly glossed bonnet. This car wouldn't need his services. It was immaculate for the year, and regularly polished.

He would have almost cleaned it for nothing.

Almost.

He looked around him. Most of the cars seemed glossier on this level. The really dirty ones, he had noticed, had been on the top floor. It was almost as though they had been grouped according to their layers of dirt.

Their mother took Julie by the hand and helped her out of the car, then slammed the door shut. The thud bounced back from the other side of the bay. They paused for a moment in order to get their bearings. Level 12 was only half full.

Their footsteps rang out as they crossed to the exit.

They were about to see the attractions of the Mall.

As the double doors opened, an alarming blast of activity hit them.

'Good God,' was Mrs Anderson's first reaction, under her breath.

The three of them stood together for a moment. They linked hands as if this might provide some protection against the chaos and commotion before them.

They had stepped out on to a wide balcony which circled an enormous indoor space. It was like overlooking an arena. The central floor was only a single flight of steps down. Around the balcony walkway was a continuous chain of shops.

Every one had open access, without shop windows or doors. Customers spilled out on to the walkway. Neon signs flashed above each one, announcing their name and, usually, the availability of credit: Laser Light Ltd: Holograms to Order (easy terms). Antrobus Electronics: Home Help in a Microchip (all credits taken).

It was only when Mrs Anderson looked up that she became aware of the impossibility of the building. Further encircling balconies and galleries stretched upwards towards the dark and distant ceiling (if indeed there was a ceiling). It was like being at the bottom of a cylinder supported by a series of broad ribs at regular intervals. Each rib consisted of row upon row of shops and stores.

The noise was tremendous. Mrs Anderson could just detect the strain of an up-tempo melody, contradicting different layers of turmoil and din.

There were people everywhere.

Frantic chatter was mixed with the squeak and crash of the trolley baskets, which were being pushed urgently round in different directions.

Occasionally, two trolleys would meet in a head-on collision, then they would reverse and continue on their way like the dodgem cars the Andersons had seen in the fun-fair centres.

Mrs Anderson tightened her grip on the children's hands. They stared around them, wide-eyed in wonder, saying nothing. A young woman pushing an overfilled trolley rushed past them. One of the wheels caught in a crack in the paving stone. She struggled to raise the frame out of the gap, wrestling for a moment with an awkward castor.

Mrs Anderson caught the look on her face. She turned cold. She had seen an expression of utter despair. The woman nervously brushed away the hair which fell in front of her face, and tears began to well in the corners of her eyes.

The trolley spilled over with unwrapped cartons. Julie caught sight of some items of interest: milk shake machines, android dolls, hologram cameras and personal video eye-sets.

'Let me help,' said Mrs Anderson, as she gently lifted the trolley. The woman stared back in astonishment. Somebody was helping her?

A large red box with a picture of a turbo food mixer fell out of the basket. The frightened look returned as the woman snatched the box up and replaced it in the trolley. She looked up again at Mrs Anderson, her lips mouthing something before she rushed away like a hunted rabbit.

Suddenly a hand caught Mrs Anderson's arm. Another face stared up into hers, but this time the anxious expression alternated with a grin. There was a young man dressed in a bright blue sweatshirt. The words CONSUMER COMFORT CLUB were written on the chest.

'It's almost "Hurry Up" time,' he said, 'and I know what it's going to be.'

His clenched fists shook with excitement. He pushed his face towards hers as if to share a secret. Beads of sweat were breaking out across his forehead.

11

'It'll be the talking towel rail. Don't tell anyone.'

He raised a finger to his lips and made a 'Shushhh', then ran off pulling two half-filled trolleys behind him.

John had once heard a book in which everybody seemed to race around getting nowhere. His mother had even shown him a picture from a real book she had had as a child, of a large-eared White Rabbit looking at a pocket watch and mumbling, 'Oh dear.' This was just like that.

Julie gently pulled her mother's sleeve.

'Come on, sweetheart,' said Mrs Anderson, 'this won't take long.' John had gone very quiet indeed. Once, when he was much younger and they lived in Manchester, his father had taken him to a meeting in Albert Square. That was before they had been advised to join the Toe-the-Line Association. The square had been packed, just like the inside of the Mall.

John had watched as all around him people's faces had grown twisted and angry. A scuffle had broken out and the Peace Police had been summoned. John and his father had been carried through the Square by the natural surge of the crowd. It had moved as a single heaving body, breaking and re-shaping, until in anger it began to turn inwards and eat itself alive.

They had been lucky to escape. Most of the crowd had later been designated Riot Zone Class, the mindless disruptive sector.

It was strange. Those in the shopping centre were Consumer Category but their faces still reminded John of Albert Square. All that anxiety.

12

His mother led them to the edge of the balcony. The ground-floor arena was just below them, a teeming mosaic of bobbing heads and crashing wire trolleys.

A tall figure in a peaked cap and blue shirt had been watching them from the car-park doors. Large drop sun-shades hid his eyes, and part of his face, but it was still possible to make out an icy, detached expression.

He had been standing against the doors with his arms folded. Now he walked towards the trolley bay, which was a confused tangle of wire mesh and thick red handles. He shook one of the trolleys free from its clinging partners and advanced on Mrs Anderson and the children. With a grunt he pushed the trolley towards them.

'Er, no. Thank you,' she stuttered, 'we only want—'

His fist crashed against the side of the basket and again he pushed the trolley at her. This time much harder. Her hands let go of the children's as she managed to catch the front edge. A loose wire caught her thumb.

'Take it! Keep on shopping, damn you!'

He hit the side of the basket again. The message was clear.

John and Julie stood quite still.

The screech of a Parade Day whistle rang round the building. Everybody froze where they stood. The air filled with whispers and urgent hushes. Even the peak cap forgot his bullying and looked upwards. A synthesised Trumpet Voluntary stabbed the air, followed by an excited female voice:

'Brought to you by the Tomorrow chain of stores, it's – HURRY UP TIME!'

The sound of a drum roll flowed into a bouncing disco beat.

There were cheers.

Above this, the voice continued its frenzied announcement.

'Even now, at this very minute, our friendly store staff at the Tomorrow chain are marking the star reduction of the hour. What will it be, folks—'

The crowd began its soft murmur, a swell of excitement surged within the mall.

'The Akoni, fully digital, talking towel rail.'

A cry of awe and wonder escaped from every mouth like the release of a pressure valve.

'And – the first dozen sold, I repeat, the first dozen only, will have the rail personalised to speak their name.'

The buzz of approval broke into pockets of discussion.

'The offer is only available in Tomorrow stores on levels 5, 7 and 12. Remember "Every Hour on the Hour with Hurry Up". Now off you go and – quiiiiickkkkly now!'

The electronic twang of a synthesised note bounced through with perfect timing, a low bass riff bringing the melody to a conclusion. An elderly woman further down the balcony cried out in an ecstatic wail:

'I MUST have one! I MUST have one!'

The shoppers broke into a mad directionless swarm.

The peaked cap man disappeared, swept away

14

like a bad dream. Mrs Anderson put her arms protectively around John and Julie as people hurried by. A burst of bongos and a chorus of silver tongues sang to a bossa nova beat:

> Can you live without your creature comforts,
> Can you afford to let good buys pass by,
> If you've a sharp eye for a bargain,
> Keep on shopping and let time drift by.
>
> Come on let's Hurry on Up.
> Quiiiickkkkkllly now!

The crowd around her responded with a cry of 'Keep on shopping!' as an army of fists shot into the air in time with the jingle.

Mrs Anderson trembled. She couldn't move, frozen with the fear of having to mingle with these people. This was evil. Pure undiluted greed.

Down on the ground floor a small group of blue-shirted men, wearing shades and peaked caps, were talking. It was obvious that they had some sort of security role. One of them looked up at her. She shivered.

They had to get out.

Julie had begun to cry. John, it seemed, had been struck dumb. He didn't know whether to laugh or not. Deep down he was fascinated.

'Now listen kids,' Mrs Anderson spoke slowly but firmly as she walked them towards the exits. 'This place isn't for us. It's too busy. Just do as Mummy says, we're going to go back to the car.'

15

The first throb of the crowd had moved on. It was now much easier to get through to the other side of the balcony. They moved amongst the anxious empty faces.

From a doorway next to the car-park doors stepped the security guard bully.

'Damn, damn,' said Mrs Anderson.

She manoeuvred John on to Julie's arm and grabbed an abandoned trolley. They changed direction, wheeling the trolley slowly towards another pair of doors set back between the first cluster of shops. Occasionally the wheels would stick in small cracks and crevices between the paving slabs. Mrs Anderson would stop and casually ease the trolley up and out of the fissure, but with eyes locked firmly on the swing doors.

Just as they passed Antrobus Electronics a large cardboard box suddenly fell into her basket. Behind the box had been a small balding man with a round pink face. He wore an outsize scruffy raincoat and his tie had been pulled up round his collar. Sweat trickled down his face as he drew breath in heavy laboured pants.

'I . . . I . . . I'm so sorry.' He struggled to regain his speech. 'I just didn't see you. I've got . . . to get this to Level 8 to deposit . . . got to. We've bought three.'

He took out a crumpled grey handkerchief from his raincoat pocket and dabbed his face. His eyes bulged, nervously trying to take in everything about him.

'It was very . . . cheap. They've still got some left

16

I think . . . Electro-land, just over there. We might even . . . be able to get a couple more with a credit disc.'

Mrs Anderson's nails dug into the red grip of the trolley. The neon shop signs began to blur and dance. She clenched her teeth, and a voice inside her head told her to hold on and act like one of them. With a blink she opened her eyes wide, becoming a talking doll.

'That's all right. I wasn't looking where I was going. What is it you've bought? It is nice, I must get one too.'

The man pushed his handkerchief deep inside his pocket and embraced the box.

'Thank you, thank you. Shopping is so good, so good. It's a CBC Television. Super "Voice Activated" in seductive ebony and pink.'

The word 'pink' was muffled by the box as it fell towards his face. He scuttled away mumbling, 'It's mine,' as he went.

Mrs Anderson wondered why he had bought three televisions and what he would do with five.

The shops on this side of the balcony all seemed to be concerned with electrical goods. Mountains of food processors, toasters, home computers and the like were neatly stacked in blocks which poured out on to the walkway. Inside the brightly lit shops eager salesmen took plastic cards, credit discs, and asked for signatures in a continual loop of:

'Certainly, sir. Top of the range. Special this week. Certainly, sir. Please sign here.'

The Andersons soon found themselves before

17

an alcove which led to yet another large pair of oval-eyed doors. Just as Mrs Anderson pushed the door inwards, a tall blonde woman with half-frame spectacles charged through from the other side. She stopped and looked directly down her nose and into the trolley. She wore a bright blue badge bearing the message 'Keep on Shopping'. She made a clicking sound with her tongue.

Piercing blue eyes held Mrs Anderson, pinning her to the spot.

'That will never do. You must do better than that. How do you expect to keep the country on its feet, eh? Tell me that. If you've run out of money it's simple, go to Level 8, two hundred credit ranges to choose from. You're privileged to be here, you know! We all have to do our bit when we first arrive. Off you go now. Keep on shopping.'

She did not have a trolley, but held a clipboard and a wedge of credit-card coupons. She vanished into the crowd.

That was it! Enough was enough.

Mrs Anderson grabbed the children by the hands and rushed through the swing doors.

They stopped dead in their tracks.

They had entered a short brightly lit corridor. There was only one way out and that was into the open mouth of a steel grey lift.

She thought quickly. They were on the bottom floor, the lift could only go up. To hell with it, they had to get out. The car could be collected later, Bob could do it. They would go straight to the exit on Level 8 and leave.

18

Mrs Anderson pushed the children into the lift, the doors closed politely behind them. She saw only one illuminated square: 8. She pressed it. They could not be certain at first that the lift was moving. It shuddered, then an increasing whine could be heard.

They were startled by a loud hiss which came from the ceiling. A tape had started which was obviously worn and ran at varying speeds.

'Hiiii therrr, since you'rrrre visiting Level 8 call in on the Credit Forever counselling centrrrrre. Unit 199. Remember, Unit 199. Keeeep orrrrn shopping.'

A fuzz of hard guitar chords and erratically crashing cymbals provided a background to another jingle:

> Credit Forever is fast and quick,
> Credit Forever will do the trick,
> Buying things is kinda' fun,
> Brings life's essentials to everyone!

At this point the cymbals wowed for several seconds and the hiss stopped.

A light above the door flashed 8.

When the lift yawned open a short corridor which mirrored the one on Level 12 greeted them. Mrs Anderson pulled the children down the passage and through the now familiar double doors. They stepped out on to another balcony.

The layout was frighteningly familiar too, but here the balcony did not overlook a central arena. Instead there was a vast space. Mrs Anderson rushed to the balcony rail and looked over.

She immediately pulled her head away.

'Oh my God,' she said, 'it's not possible, do they go on for ever?'

She looked up.

Everything swam.

Above her she counted seven huge concrete bands, each bustling with noise and activity. These were Levels 7 to 1, capped by a huge dark blue dome which seemed to sit above the last balcony. Again she looked down. She could make out other balconies and shopping chains. Lights flashed from the shops and various jingles spilled over into the abyss. Shafts of light crossed from one level to another. Many projected down and down and down.

It had to be an optical effect.

A blue-sleeved arm pulled her from the rail. She cried out as she caught her reflection in a large pair of drop shades.

'Are you all right? We don't want any "leapers". Ruins the shopping for some,' he said.

He grinned, revealing a pattern of brilliant white and gold teeth (a Government perk). They alternated perfectly.

'Do you want credit?'

He nodded towards the long row of counters. The Andersons had stopped where the electrical shops had been on Level 12.

Mrs Anderson swallowed and wiped her nose on her sleeve.

'No, no thank you. Where is the exit, please?'

The grin vanished. The face said nothing for a moment.

'The exit?'

'Yes! Yes.'

He did not seem to understand the question. Then the teeth appeared again.

'Oh, you mean the exit to the levels. To and from.'

'*Yes*,' she agreed, nodding furiously, 'the exits!'

She would nod at anything. She just wanted to get away.

'Well, that's easy. Through those doors. That'll get you through to the lanes.'

He pointed to a pair of yellow doors set back from the front of a Consumer Comfort Bank. Through the oval eyes she could make out the dim glow of the car-park lighting.

She mouthed a word of thanks and pulled the children. John's arm resisted the tug. She looked round. He was looking up at the guard. A smile glowed from his face.

'Keep on shopping,' he said.

The guard smiled back.

They were the first words that John had spoken.

Julie laughed and repeated the words.

'Yes! Keep on shopping!' Then she giggled coyly.

'Nice kids,' said the guard.

Mrs Anderson's heart leapt into her mouth. She almost gagged. She pulled harder, dragging the children towards the oval eyes of the doors. A voice called out behind her.

'Hey! The lift is easier, you know!'

Once through the double swing doors she fell back against the wall and closed her eyes. She shook with sobs as the sound echoed mockingly back across the car park.

Through the tears came distorted shapes and colours. The sign she had noticed when they had first arrived was still there.

But there was something wrong with it.

YOUR PIECE OF MIND IS OUR PIECE OF MIND.

There were signs that indicated DOWN to Level 9, or UP to Level 7. Signs that indicated which EXIT lane led to which level. Signs that told you where the lift or EXIT to the balcony was. But there was nothing which read WAY OUT, or just plain EXIT.

She began to take the EXIT lane to Level 9.

The children walked behind her, perfectly in step.

Their eyes were glazed and they smiled, quietly humming 'Credit Forever'.

Twenty minutes later they were all sitting in the car. Mrs Anderson crouched over the steering wheel. The air was hot and sticky. Had the storm finished? She was trying to remain calm, but it was difficult. She had driven back up to Level 8, but everything looked different and she had been unable to find a way out. The car had somehow got into the wrong lane.

They were now at Level 10 having already been to the top and back. There must be another route out. Level 12 had to lead to a special exit lane, she had heard of something similar in the south-western multi-storeys. You had to drive through all the floors to get out. That must be it, mustn't it?

She pushed the accelerator down to the floor. The engine screamed.

She bit down hard on her tongue, her eyes fixed on the LEVEL 11 arrow.

With a roar the car catapulted down the ramp to Level 11.

Tyres tore as the white estate sought Level 12.

Almost unconsciously the car discovered EXIT TO LEVEL 13.

'Level 13?' she gasped.

Then she laughed.

And the children laughed.

Radio Mall One was really quite good after a while. It was the only radio station which the car's receiver would pick up, but that was perfectly understandable, being in a huge concrete car park.

There would be lots of 'give-away' prizes with the hologram photograph demonstration at 7 p.m. on Level 2. She thought that sounded like fun.

There would also be free Radio Mall One T-shirts. Her hands were dry, her eyes bright and shining.

After an hour they had all learnt the words to the Hurry Up Song:

'Can you live without your creature comforts?'

A pretty tune. All three had sung it together, Julie had even made up a new verse. They would send that in.

They also knew the salute to 'Keep on shopping'.

Might as well carry on until the petrol ran out. Curiosity really. A shopping Mall could be so welcoming. So warm.

After they left the EXIT lane from Level 50, the car slipped on to Level 1 again.
    And again . . .

Home Improvements

Abigail Fletcher hated Saturdays.

'Of course, a reduced power consumption will always be an advantage. These new improved circuits run much cooler. You see, there is no longer any need for the bonding together of transistors.'

The eyebrows rose as if to say, 'How about that then?'

The pipe was removed from beneath a grey bushy moustache and a polite laugh, perhaps a snigger, slid easily out of the mouth of W. Gordon, 'Personal Consultant' for hi-fi installation.

'Believe it or not, there are some who can't tell any difference in sound quality.'

W. Gordon looked as smug as a fat tom cat.

'Amaaazing, fancy not being able to notice the improvement,' said Russell.

W. Gordon's eyes rolled upwards as he tutted and shook his head.

'But you've got good ears, Russell,' continued W. Gordon, 'we know this, you are a SPECIAL customer, a DISCERNING customer. The earlier pre-amps had the series 3B boards which, as we all know, produced a certain haziness, lack of resolution. Poor imaging and of course *such* a high power consumption. Disaster really.'

The moment was right.

Hooked.

W. Gordon slipped into sales mode, matter-of-fact gear:

'As you have the earlier model, we would be willing to part exchange or you could easily upgrade the existing unit with the simple modular plug-in circuit boards. These easily fit into the original mother boards by simply removing three screws at the base of the unit and replacing the series 49D mother board with our own newer version (we are the only shop to provide this service – a little thing we do for our much valued customers). We only charge £349 + VAT for this which is exactly what our engineer, Roger, charges us, so we don't actually accrue any personal benefit from this at all, but we do like to look after our customers and would hate to sell you anything which would just be redundant after a few months' use. The usual chain stores, of course, just don't want to know you after you walk away with a nicely sealed and unchecked carton, but we at W. Gordon & Son pride ourselves in making sure that you will return to us time and time again.'

W. Gordon paused.

'Buying hi-fi can be such a personal experience.'

He stopped suddenly, it was as if he had been unplugged, and gazed into a cloud of pipe smoke.

'Amaaazing,' said Russell, 'I suppose being a hi-fi consultant is like being a doctor, so much responsibility.'

The pipe re-entered the mouth. The head nodded sagely.

There was always a certain dignity surrounding a business transaction with W. Gordon & Son.

Russell too had been nodding rapidly in agreement. At £349 + VAT it was a gift.

'Quite obviously I have to have it,' he said, 'in fact we'd be selling ourselves short if we didn't buy it. I mean having such an excellent unit which is capable of so much more.'

The bowl of the pipe gently rose and fell in polite assent. 'Here is a man who has ears,' thought W. Gordon, 'who can see sense and who spends money.'

The sale was closed.

Russell would write the cheque *now* – just to be sure that he wouldn't have to wait once the units were delivered to the shop.

Abigail, Russell's young wife of three months, struggled with the two large plastic carrier bags of shopping. Her heart sank as she watched the two men titter and guffaw pompously about a customer in the nearby demonstration room.

He wanted to buy a cheap music centre!

A music centre from W. Gordon & Son!

Great gods! Gordon's was a QUALITY shop, not a discount store!

Russell wrote the cheque, but after a moment of quick calculation, tore it up. With much apologising he handed his Bonuscard to a slightly cooler W. Gordon, who looked down his nose at the plastic card. Credit cards! How ungentlemanly! He would have to pay commission on the sale.

They crossed the 'listening area' to the reproduction Georgian desk. W. Gordon looked for the machine to process the piece of plastic. He handled the card with some disdain, even disgust. He preferred the old-fashioned ways. Most customers were 'cash'.

Russell thanked W. Gordon, held out his clammy hand and disappeared with a final nasal 'Amaaazing'.

The neon lights of Computer Fair burned brightly. High tech box-shifting-razzmatazz.

'Mr Fletcher, hey, it's so fabby to see yer. How's the missus? Mary, Annie?'

'Abigail actually,' grinned Russell.

The salesman winked at his colleague, a pimply youth.

'Thought you'd have traded her in for a new model, eh, eh?'

The salesman beamed.

'Are we glad to see you, me old mate! You ain't going to believe this. Have we got a surprise for *you*!'

Russell had just got through the door. His wet hair sat flat and shiny as rain drops dripped on to the floor from the tip of his nose. He stood framed within the shop lobby. A stupid smile spread from ear to ear as he tried to guess what this surprise could be.

Behind him Abigail still battled with the carrier bags. The door had closed in her face, leaving her to the mercy of the never-ending downpour. It had been his idea that they 'take shelter in Computer Fair – just until the rain cleared. Just to have a quick look round.'

Russell crossed the showroom floor to the young man. The salesman had been leaning casually against the glass counter. This was quite a different shop. It was a magical playground, perhaps a little brusque and not at all like the conservative and quite gentlemanly W. Gordon & Son, but fun.

Hard lighting burned down on to a dazzling display of televisions, VDUs and keyboards. There were rows and rows of them, each grouped in perfectly matched families with accompanying sales cards. Each card claimed *that* system to be the best available within its price range. There were huge unrepeatable discounts and they all seemed to be the special buy of the week.

It was a busy shop: bleeps of ERROR resounded throughout the foyer, intermingling with the sound of angry buzzers triggered off when a computer game target had been missed. There were synthesised voice commands, gargling out instructions, punctuating the drone of customer chatter. As always there were lines of eager young faces staring relentlessly into the glare of multi-coloured screens. The antics of cartoon warriors were reflected in the pupils of their wide, admiring eyes.

The smart young man wearing the red and white 'in house' store blazer was removing the dirt from under his finger-nails, using the tip of a Computer Fair give-away ballpoint pen.

'Am I right in thinking that this here gentleman is one of our special customers who own an X720 Wazuti personal computer?'

Russell laughed.

'Go ooonnnn. You know I am.'

'Well,' continued the salesman, 'we, Computer Fair, exclusive to us, mind you, have just taken delivery of a limited number of the new "Add-On Kits" for the disc drive. An extra 720K, IBM compatible at a price which is simply ridiculous!'

Russell almost swooned.

'Amaaaaaaaaazing!'

His heartbeat quickened. He had been waiting for this and had spent the last month ringing round everywhere to find it, from Newcastle to Penzance. Russell's embarrassingly nasal voice was famous.

Abigail couldn't understand why he needed the extra unit. He wasn't completely certain himself, but he'd been assured by all the magazines that the unit, when it became available, was a MUST.

It was all too technical for Abigail.

The salesman looked up and displayed the perfect sales smile, spoilt only by a chipped front incisor.

'Only got a few in, me old mate.'

'I'll have one,' snapped Russell, reaching for his Bonuscard.

The salesman made a signal to a younger red-coated figure who quickly disappeared downstairs to the stockroom.

'You may have to wait a few minutes, as they've

only just come in. The consignment's probably still being checked and they've got a new boy downstairs. Between you and me he's a wally of the first order,' said the salesman.

A new brochure for Russell's make of computer lay on the shop counter. Hungrily he scanned the announcements of forthcoming models: an entire new Wazuti range.

'Amaaazing,' exclaimed Russell, 'the interface unit is now a standard item rather than an optional extra!'

'Of course,' said the salesman, looking up from his sales pad.

Russell had to give it to them, clever marketing. Eight new models were due out, but why wasn't his own listed? The phone on the counter rang and the sales smile clicked into place.

'Wouldn't you know it!' The salesman's eyes rolled upwards.

Russell was shaken out of his technological dream by the salesman's angry voice.

'That was the stockroom. Bleedin' importers. All the units are single complicity to configuration RT54443.'

Russell blinked.

'Does that mean they're no good?' he asked.

'Well, of course they're no bloody good, you pillock. (Only joking.) The X720 needs dual complicity and to RS54443 in bog standard American International Interchange mode. Unless—'

Russell swallowed as the salesman sank into a trancelike moment of deep thought.

'Unless you interface the RT54443 with an exchange

buffer of RS code such as the VXU100. That should do it nicely, don't you think, and it would be useful if you needed to take the machine abroad with you, to Japan for example.'

'Do you have one?' asked Russell.

The salesman picked up the telephone and rattled a gobbledegook of serial numbers down to the stockroom. He raised two crossed fingers. After a few moments he grinned once again.

'Yes, we've just got one left, but it's an extra £89.99—'

'Amaaaaazing!' said Russell. 'It doesn't matter. I must have it.'

In the doorway a rain-drenched Abigail waited patiently with the carrier bags.

The pimply youth made a rude gesture with his hand behind Russell's back.

On their way home Russell bought a copy of *Photography for Tomorrow*. Once settled on their crowded bus he opened the magazine and began to scan the special offers and upgrade page.

'Abigail,' he shouted suddenly.

The bus went quiet. Abigail stood in the aisle with the dripping carriers.

'Simply-simply, absolutely, amaaaazing,' continued Russell, 'there's an unrepeatable offer for an add-on Cheenon B25 lens filter. An exclusive offer *only* for readers of *Photography for Tomorrow*. It says here that it's an essential device for taking photographs in desert regions where the glare of the sun on sand makes reflection a problem. It's important for Arctic region photography too.'

How could he live without it?

Russell's finger shot to the stop button and pushed hard until the bus screeched to a halt. Abigail fell against the other passengers.

'Come on, come on, there's a phone box across the road!'

With a curse from the conductor Russell and Abigail were let off the bus. Russell couldn't wait. He would telephone the order through. He might even receive the lens the next day.

Russell and Abigail waited an hour for the next bus.

It was still raining and one of the carrier-bag handles had snapped. The other bag was about to snap too.

So was Abigail.

The bus dropped them at the bottom of the drive which led to the Barlow's Honey Homes estate. Large yellow signposts pointed the way to Showhouses, open 9 to 5 and 10 to 4 on Sundays.

On either side of the estate drive there were large heaps of gravel, sand and cement. The upper handle of a lone shovel protruded from the centre of one of the mounds.

Ropes and red pointed cones cordoned off large sections of the road. Solitary cement mixers stood by abandoned trucks.

Behind this collection of hardware, windows in red-brick walls proclaimed SOLD and FOR SALE. Completion of the estate seemed to be taking ages to Abigail. She would be glad when they could just get home without having to go through an obstacle course.

Their little town house was sandwiched between two 'Swiss Chalet' style constructions, still awaiting the genuine Alpine woodcarving feature which was to adorn their front porches.

Russell bounded up the front path with Abigail wavering behind like a drunk penguin. The carrier bags were somehow getting heavier and she now had a strange buzzing noise in her head.

The improved burglar alarm system still had to be negotiated. Opening the front door was not a completely straightforward procedure. It didn't matter too much because Russell was so good at it, although the careful insertion of a piece of metal foil before turning the lock was tricky, but essential if you didn't want the entire neighbourhood to realise that you had twelve klaxons, four alarm bells and a direct line to the two local police stations. After being called out for the fourth time the local Crime Prevention Officer had had to be physically restrained by the Duty Sergeant.

Abigail often had to wait outside for Russell to let her in if she was home early from work.

Once inside the house they were greeted by the smell of newly laid carpet. Offcuts of foam-rubber underlay and empty plastic wrapping were scattered around the hallway.

Russell had initially thought that the new carpet would be a vast improvement on the simple contract cord which had been a free standard item with the house. After only two weeks he was rushing around the shops in desperate search for a better carpet, one which would be more in keeping with his home's individuality.

He had gone very quiet after the fitter had left.

Abigail had discovered matching labels on the back of the offcuts. Russell had bought the same carpet as had been supplied with the house. Russell's face had furrowed into an angry frown.

'They're not the same,' he'd said. 'They can't be. I know these showhouses. Inferior quality. The old carpet was a "second". Any fool can see that.'

Abigail couldn't see any difference.

Russell went quiet. He was slipping into one of his moods.

Abigail sloped off and quietly collapsed in a heap on the stairs. The buzzing in her head had turned into a headache.

Russell went straight to the kitchen to see if the glue had dried on his own modification to the Danish luxury Heeldebourn range of kitchen units. He would feel better if he continued with a little DIY.

The addition of a tasteful imitation pine strip to the top of the units had considerably improved their appearance.

If only the glue would stick.

In the corner of the kitchen lay a pile of original Danish brass door handles. Nasty, mass-produced stuff. They would be replaced by hand-carved 'cottage mouldings'. He had had these specially made by a small firm he'd found in the *Market and Exchange* magazine. They'd be here soon.

Russell tentatively pressed the pine strip to see if it had taken. Slowly, it slid to an oblique angle.

Abigail suddenly appeared in the doorway, carriers at the end of her arms, making her a pair of human kitchen scales. She stared around her.

Home improvements! Home improvements and Saturdays!

Saturdays were grey for her, they were Russell's shopping days. She was terrified of them, and they had been getting worse.

Nothing but nothing was ever good enough as it was.

Simply thinking about it all made her tense and edgy. She spent Fridays psychologically adjusting to the fact that as sure as the sun would rise, Saturday would follow.

Abigail started to shake. She had to get out. The walls were closing in on her. The ceiling pressed down.

It would help to lie down but she could not even do that. Upstairs, their mattress was propped against the bedroom door: the legs of the bed had been shortened unequally. This had been Russell's attempt at 'customising' the bedroom furniture. Create a new height. Russell had thought it irritating that there always seemed to be one leg which turned out to be much shorter than the others, no matter how many times the others were cut back to length. A three-foot-high bed now stood at ten inches with a sloping angle to the upper right-hand corner.

The hall was cluttered with furniture and various

items of electronic equipment. The insides of numerous videos were piled on top of TV sets and aluminium boxes formed short but unsteady towers. These contained special add-on units which improved reception, produced quadraphonic sound and would receive satellite television when it arrived. Most of the equipment had been taken out of its casing, victim of Russell's modifications.

Russell continued to work at his kitchen. He held the obstinate pine strip with one finger whilst balancing a hammer and packet of tacks with his free hand.

'Abigail!'

No reply. She'd left the room.

'Abigail! I can't do it all dear, you really should pull your weight.'

At first he thought he heard the soft sound of the hum of a lullaby, then the click of the latch on the front door.

He struggled with the stubborn strip. It was no use, assistance was required, he couldn't do everything.

Russell returned to the hall.

She had gone.

'T-y-p-i-c-a-l!' he exclaimed, 'a-m-a-a-a-a-z-i-n-g! I bet she's gone off on one of her walks!'

He peered through the hall window and saw a small solitary figure in a patterned headscarf shuffle across the recreation lawn opposite. It had stopped raining now, but in her baggy brown raincoat and with her bent head he thought Abigail looked a rather pitiful figure. Even old.

'Such a weak woman,' he muttered, 'I must find time to improve her.'

Russell sat cross-legged in the middle of the lounge floor.

He had been getting nowhere in the kitchen and it was beginning to irritate him. There was still the hi-fi to set up.

Behind him was a single black leather armchair. His stereo loudspeakers looked out from the corners of the room. In the last two hours they had been in twenty-seven different positions and in every permutation they had sounded wrong.

First he had placed them with their backs to the walls, then he tried them a few feet from the new false wall (which Russell had installed as an acoustic baffler). The speaker stands each had four sharp spikes on their base. This had been an enormously beneficial 'tuning tip': much tighter bass, good solid imaging and an *amaaazing* soundstage.

Spikes were now on everything. The turntable, the amplifier, the chair and even the television. Tightened everything up!

But somehow it no longer sounded *quite* right.

The bass was soggy, the instruments were difficult to place and identify and he had moved his armchair so many times that he'd become dizzy.

Russell sighed. It was so hard to live. Then something occurred to him.

It must be the new carpet. It couldn't be anything else!

'Come on, Russell lad,' he said to himself, 'give it

a bit of a rest. Everything will fit neatly in its place later. Sort something else out.'

He looked about him. Pieces of the TV and video were scattered across the floor. He would re-install them in their special place.

'Their place' was not really ready yet. Last month Russell had read in *Video News* that all kinds of unwanted electrical static built up within a television casing, significantly interfering (the article claimed) with the quality of the picture.

Within thirty minutes he had had the TV chassis out of its casing. This had been the point at which the usually accommodating Abigail had put her foot down and shaken her head. The woman had no vision, no experimental spirit. But last weekend Russell had implemented his brilliant plan while Abigail was at her mother's.

That was the point when she seemed to have turned a bit funny. But things *did* work better out of their casings! He had proved that with other domestic electrical goods.

In one corner of the room was a gaping hole. It had been easy, the walls were only constructed of plasterboard – they were hollow. The TV would be fitted into the wall. How could he have known that there would be a structural beam behind all that plaster? The temporary shelf suited the purpose and held the beams in position. He would just try and get the TV into the gap. It would be a surprise. Abigail would be pleased.

He'd have to make a new hole.

The speakers were obstructing the view, it would

be a simple matter to fill in the old gap. He quite liked the idea of a central viewing point anyway. It was a pity (and plain bad luck) that he had found brickwork half-way up – that had been a surprise.

He laughed quietly to himself when he remembered that he hadn't really satisfactorily decided where his speakers should go anyway.

He returned to the kitchen and made a cup of tea. He stared at the stubborn pine strip. Russell weighed the pros and cons.

Kitchen, video, hi-fi?

The speakers were important. He listened to a lot of music, sometimes, when the equipment was installed and working. But usually the hi-fi was being modified or awaiting a new part for an upgrade.

He thought about this long and hard while he drank his tea.

'Come on, Russell,' he said to himself, 'take courage. It's no good having an expensive hi-fi if you're not going to be able to appreciate its full potential.'

W. Gordon's would be having the upgrade for the pre-amplifier soon. He licked his lips in anticipation. A man had to do what a man had to do. It could sound amaaazing.

The imaging *was* amazing. He could almost reach out and touch the instruments. He would ring W. Gordon and invite him round one evening, he wouldn't believe how good his system now sounded.

Abigail would agree, of course.

40

He decided on another cuppa, as a reward. He stepped over the pile of ripped carpet which cluttered the hallway.

In the kitchen the new pine strip had slipped again and was stuck solidly at an angle of forty-five degrees.

Russell tutted.

Gently he eased the strip away from the unit surface.

Very gradually the top of the work surface peeled away revealing flecks of light brown woodchip. He could not believe it – he would be writing to the site manager, he expected the units to be 'quality', not this. It had been a lucky stroke to discover the fault through his creative design modification. He decided to leave the job until he could arrange to get it inspected. If they agreed the right price he could perhaps get some better units installed.

Russell went back into the lounge. Large patches of underlay remained, a sea of rubber islands stuck to the floor. They would have to think of some alternative floor covering which would allow the spiked speaker stands to achieve their potential. For a moment he considered the idea of sanding the floor and adding a couple of coats of varnish.

His imagination ran riot. They could have an open-plan effect. Carry the concept through. He had seen the idea in the weekend colour supplements. A dull ordinary lounge floor became a sea of high-quality yacht varnish in superior gloss.

He stood back against the rear wall. Cupping each ear with a hand he shouted and then stamped his foot. The acoustics weren't bad, but . . . Another idea! The removal of part of the rear wall would allow an 0.8 second delay and the reverb would enhance the sound. In fact, he could convert the system to four speakers and then add another amplifier. Quadraphonic sound. But properly installed, of course. W. Gordon would advise.

'It must be done,' said Russell, 'it could sound amaa—'

He decided to test an area.

Part of the back wall would have to come out. A matrix system. He could even make it encoded! Rear speakers could take up the signals from the additional amplifier and if they were properly linked up with the television set then it would be possible to produce proper cinema Dolby encoded quadraphonic surround sound.

'Amaaaazing!' said Russell.

It was late afternoon and Russell sat in the leather armchair. A mallet lay in his lap and the extra light came through from the dining room next door. The rear wall had three large ragged holes, opening into the lounge.

Plaster dust and chunks of brick were everywhere, speaker cables all over the floor. It was impossible to tell what went where.

But he felt happy, seated in a pool of live spaghetti.

The latch turned in the front lock. A small childlike voice sang a nursery rhyme. The la-la-la floated through to the lounge.

Abigail stood in the doorway, her head about to burst.

Police Cadet Barrow was still in a state of shock.

The Desk Sergeant had sat him down with a cup of strong coffee, and mumbled something about 'Welcome to the force'. They had all joked when the radio message came. The Fletcher burglar-alarm system had gone off again at the Honey Homes estate. During the drive there PC Jenkins had explained that they had a 'right one' at this house, but they were obliged to check it out just the same.

He couldn't believe what they found. He still felt queasy just thinking about it.

The front door had been wide open. Mrs Fletcher was sitting on the front step giggling and singing something. He remembered one or two of the words, about a bird. Was it a song about a mockingbird?

Detective Sergeant Phillips said that he had never encountered anything like it before.

'Bizarre' was the word he used.

They had found Mrs Fletcher's husband in the lounge. Attempts had been made to glue several strips of pine veneer on to his body. Barrow could not understand why Mr Fletcher had been propped up in the chair in such an odd way. He seemed to be floating there, his head all floppy and his feet resting on a crooked pair of six-inch spikes: they looked like nails with their heads clipped off.

When Detective Sergeant Phillips and the doctor

43

from HQ arrived they found the hole in the middle of his chest. A red mass of bloody wires and electrical cable tumbled out. Bits of solder and circuit boards, followed by din plugs and a couple of floppy discs, fell on to the floor. There were also what one policeman thought might be computer microchips. The components were good. Quality upgrade hardware and there were even one or two of the new RS2339Z motorola chips!

Suddenly the interview room door opened. Phillips came out, slowly shaking his head.

'Has she said anything yet, sir?' asked Barrow.

'Yes,' came the reply, 'she's said something at last, but I don't know that I understand it. Something about wanting to "upgrade" her husband? Improve him, she said. Give him more RAM? Another disc drive? Give him better imaging? I don't know what she means. I'll try again later. Said she wanted to carry out modifications, to please him.'

Barrow thought for a moment. It didn't make sense.

He shivered. He'd never forget one sight in particular. The memory made him swallow hard.

They had thought it was a vase at first, but it wasn't: Mr Fletcher's bleached white skull had sat prominently on a shelf in one of the ragged holes in the rear wall.

'The head, did she explain why?'

Phillips sniffed as he turned.

44

'Oh yes, she did say something about that. Don't know that you'd call it an explanation though. What was it? "Static electricity was interfering with him, it was better out of its casing. The improvement was amazing." '

The Hologram
of Uncle Emilio

For Ennio Morricone

At the last count Aunt Edda had filled her home with thirty-two deceased relatives. All of the Nicolai family had been crammed into the second-floor bedroom (they were on Mama's side of the family).

The third-floor reception had a couple of Ciprianis with the recent addition of Gianni the dog – who wasn't dead yet, but completed the collection nicely.

Uncle Bruno (also still alive – but he had given his consent), was reunited with his great-grandfather and a solitary Fabrizi in the laundry room.

Then there were the gunfighters of course. They were everywhere.

Mario's mama had always said:

'Your Aunt Edda – she crazy. The screw – she loose!'

It had seemed to Mario that he had been hearing comments such as this all his life. Even though he had never known his aunt particularly well, she had

47

figured in his relatives' conversation for as long as he could remember.

Free advice from Mama, of course, had always been around:

'Get rid of the house Edda, she too big now the *bambini* are gone!'

'Never. Where I put my friends – where I put the family?' Aunt Edda had replied.

'Edda – you a-crazy, you know that, a-crazy!'

The first indication of Aunt Edda's love of gadgets had been her purchase of a spaghetti counter from Antrobus Electronics. When dinnertime came she could tell you how many strands were in the pot and even the average length and circumference of each piece.

Not only could she tell you, she *did* tell you, every time spaghetti was served.

'That piece there, she thirty centimetres. Who'd a-thought it? You eat her all up. OK. Good for you.'

Uncle Emilio's lasagne, for years lovingly baked in a clay dish on a long setting, just as his papa's before him, was suddenly regurgitated from a microwave. That was the beginning of the end, according to Mama. That was what had sent Uncle Emilio to an early grave.

That and Edda's high-tech habits.

The family had always been relieved that Emilio had been left alone. Until now there had been no talk of a resurrection. However, after ten years, his soul having happily rested in peace undisturbed, Aunt Edda had announced the decision to add him to the ever-increasing ensemble. She had formally advertised this on a printed card to close family and friends. Mario was to have the honour of being the first to visit.

Time had passed and to some extent healed, so now she thought that she could face having Emilio around without bursting into tears every few minutes.

Mario had never seen Uncle Emilio before, not even a photograph. Mama had claimed that she could remember a visit from Emilio when Mario was just a *bambino*.

Emilio's romance with Aunt Edda had been the talk of the family at the time. Emilio was crazy about the movies and just as crazy about Aunt Edda. Edda had been a pretty girl in those days, before the layers of pasta and the furrows of a well-lived life had begun to show. Emilio had been a projectionist at the little cinema in San Lorenzo, where she was a regular customer. Five hundred lira's worth of ice cream, a double bill and a passionate row about the films of Fellini in the pizzeria afterwards.

That was living. They had been made for each other.

Uncle Emilio was legendary, so, quite naturally, Aunt Edda's invitation to the installation was eagerly received. Mario had only been to her house once before. It had been an adventure.

In memory of Uncle Emilio she had had the final gunfight scene from *A Fistful of Dollars* put into the ground-floor kitchen, just by the dishwasher. He used to re-run that scene after all the customers had left the little cinema in Via Casa. Uncle Emilio had loved his spaghetti Westerns and Ennio Morricone's music!

Once he had got used to the fact that there was no need to duck when he stood at the sink or made the *cappuccino*, it was really no inconvenience at all.

Aunt Edda had always wanted to put Uncle Emilio in the scene with Gian-Maria Volonte, or a triple gunfight with Clint Eastwood and Lee Van Cleef. Let them all shoot it out together! Laser Light Ltd had said it was technically rather difficult, but they would let her know. After all, everything was possible with lasers.

The first visit to Aunt Edda's could be very confusing.

From the outside it looked like an ordinary small house, pretty run-of-the-mill.

But not inside.

Edda had spent a fortune getting rid of silicon plastic wall covering and the 'new' comfy mould furniture. She simply transformed the place into a home for her fondest memories. A proper home, the Italy of Sophia Loren, Federico Fellini and Sergio Leone. The Italy of Edda and Emilio.

The impression was now that of the older traditional Italian house, of the 1950s or 1960s: ceramic tiling, marble, relics of Our Lady and much ornamentation. Edda had even ordered some special decor from Rome. Usually there would be hundreds of photographs of the family, just as in the old days,

50

but it was on this feature that Aunt Edda had been able to go one better. The 'high-tech' touch.

She had seen the 'devices' on sale in the Mall, a special promotion. She'd bought only a single unit at first. Now they were everywhere.

It was a school holiday when Mario went to visit. The taxi had dropped him directly at the house, from the station, and he badly needed to attend to a call of nature.

Mario was about to meet the family.

It was while in the first-floor bathroom that the Colossus of Rhodes had unexpectedly flickered into life just by the shower. A huge bearded man, dressed in chains and sackcloth. It had given Mario quite a turn.

He also found himself saying 'Excuse me' when he met distant relatives in the corridors. Then he remembered that being holograms all he had to do was walk through them. Ignoring the huge belly of Uncle Franco was easier said than done, though. All the images were startlingly, frighteningly real.

Aunt Edda explained that the feedback mechanism had been modified since his last trip. It was a long story not worth telling.

To a new visitor the house appeared to be filled with security cameras. But they were better than that. They were the laser guns which fired the hologram images down into the room, projecting Edda's private army. The small black tubes were all over the house. Usually the devices hung on

51

brackets from the ceiling. They peered down like a strange species of insect, crouching and waiting as if they would suddenly scurry down the wall at the first opportunity.

'Why I need alarms – I have the whole family, gunfighters and the Colossus of Rhodes. I tell you, no one will come into my bathroom without the OK! Al Capone? He is in the shed!'

'She is crazy! Everywhere, gangsters, movie stars, old-time and new-time!' Mama's words sprang to Mario's mind yet again.

It was not nearly as crowded as the last time he had visited, although there were now far more hologram images installed. This, apparently, was because of yet another modification.

The actual materialisation was now staggered, images would appear at random, quite unexpectedly sometimes, but this was so that Edda could get more into the house.

Aunt Edda had been upgrading her system at every opportunity, but there had been problems with recent upgrades. Aunt Milva had materialised inside Clint Eastwood one afternoon. That had been nasty, so the laser light company were called out yet again. It had been the third time that month that something had gone wrong.

Now, of course, there was another problem.

Mario was here and Uncle Emilio wasn't.

'It is no good, Mario,' said Aunt Edda, 'I pay much money for only the best. I do all they ask. I pick the best photograph I have of your uncle. I fill out the form an' say I want a hologram of my Emilio

– the 'andsome one in the photograph. I send. *Niente!* Nothing!'

Mario nodded in silence. Aunt Edda was waving her arms around in dramatic emphasis. She reminded him of an opera singer.

From the corner of the room something fizzed and crackled inside a small wall-mounted box. Cousin Francesco materialised by the dresser. The image shimmered for a few moments: a distant mirage across the living room. Cousin Francesco turned around, a vase fell from the corner of the dresser shelf. It smashed on to the marble tiles, a hundred tiny pieces scattered across the floor.

Cousin Francesco grinned and then folded in on himself, vanishing as quickly as he had appeared.

'Not again,' said Aunt Edda, 'you see that, Mario? As a-clear as day. Your second cousin, he come, smash my vase, and go!'

Mario was confused. Holograms were supposed to be light, how could a three-dimensional image physically move a real object?

'The man. He come two weeks ago,' continued Aunt Edda. 'Not to worry, he tell me. It is the feedback bit, she go wrong. No problems, just extra . . . extra . . . what was the word . . . ah – REALITY, yes *reality* in the laser gun. Sometimes the image will be more solid, my modification, you see, it is not quite right yet. So now, sometimes, if some of my family, they come and say hello they also smasha the house up if they appear inside an object.'

Aunt Edda's face suddenly shone.

'Do you mean they come to life?' asked Mario.

His eyes widened in expectation. This sounded exciting.

Aunt Edda had a complicated way of explaining things and being the Englishman in the family made it difficult for him to follow everything she said.

'I think so,' continued Aunt Edda in a hushed voice, 'but listen. I pretend to be mad about the problem but secretly I 'ave a plan. Just for fun! So I say: "No need to rush to fix it, but this, this IS very urgent. I give you the picture of my Emilio. Make-a the image. I want a-special, get it back to me specially quick." So I give a good picture, it is your Uncle out-a side his cinema. He looks so handsome.'

A cunning smile began to spread across her face.

'To myself I say: to be able to 'old that man once more in my arms if only for a moment . . . *Bellissimo.*'

Bellissimo.

Aunt Edda lifted her thumb and forefinger and slowly plucked a kiss from her lips. A rosy glow lit her cheeks. Now Mario understood the change of heart, why there had been such a sudden decision to have a hologram made of Uncle Emilio.

It was to be a romantic reunion.

Meanwhile, in the corner of the room the wall-control box fizzed again as Cousin Francesco's image rippled into view once more, a small balding man who fell against the wall knocking a picture of St Peter from its hook.

'*Buongiorno!* '

A tiny, distant voice could just be located somewhere within the image. Aunt Edda threw her hands up in horror. Within seconds she was at the control box. She pushed a button numbered 9: a square shiny plate of glass slid out of the side of the unit.

The laser gun above them let out an 'engaged' click and Cousin Francesco dissolved.

'It is bad enough that Francesco smash the vase. But-a to talk to him would be impossible. So boring, *Mama mia!* That man . . . you would not believe it!'

Aunt Edda placed the hologram plate on the small coffee table and picked up the broken picture. Cautiously Mario lifted the shiny square of glass and held it up to the light. A grinning face sat on top of a generously proportioned human outline. That was Cousin Francesco all right.

'How do they do it?' Mario asked.

'Don't ask me. I send a photograph. Back she comes with a little piece of glass and a very big a-bill. If you look at the original photo then you see a little orange ring around the person you want-a the hologram of. That is where they have lifted the image, and that is what you get!'

Mario stared at the plate in wonder. His school had just installed a new three-dimensional television. It would not be long before everybody could afford laser pictures, but nobody had a collection quite like Aunt Edda's.

Nobody. Thank goodness.

* * *

By the third day of his visit Mario had to admit that he was getting bored. Being a kid from out of town he stayed indoors. Laser Light Ltd had still not delivered Uncle Emilio and the increasing problem of the intermittent solidity fault, as it was called, had caused Aunt Edda to shut the system down temporarily. (Things came to a head when Lee Van Cleef almost shot Mario as he fetched the parmesan cheese for the spaghetti bolognese.)

Aunt Edda just wanted one more opportunity to hold her beloved Emilio again and then she would let the engineers rectify the fault in the projection system. Mario found the idea very moving, but the myth and legend of Uncle Emilio had fired his impatience. What did Emilio look like? Perhaps they might even hear him speak! But there were only three days of his holiday left.

On the afternoon of the last day there was a knock at the door. A quick peek through the viewfinder revealed a tall young man in a pair of gleaming white overalls and a peaked cap. He turned away from the door and began to whistle – the Creature Comforts Mall song which Mario had heard everywhere. On his back it said: LASER LIGHT – DOMESTIC SERVICE CONSUMER COMFORT SHOPPING MALL, in large coloured letters.

Uncle Emilio had arrived.

Mario could hardly contain his excitement. He opened the door.

'Package for Mrs E. Morello, please?' asked the young man.

'She's at the Shopping Mall,' said Mario, 'won't

be back until this evening, but it's all right, I'm her nephew.'

The man looked down at Mario, sucking in his breath as he lifted his cap and scratched his head.

'This has to be signed for, it's special.'

'It's all right, really it is. It's our hologram, the one of Uncle, we've been waiting ages for it.'

'It's against company regs, you've got to be careful you know, we can't hand these over to just anyone.'

The man thought for a moment. It was one of the last deliveries for that area. If he dropped it off he could pop home for a cup of tea.

'Righteeo then, son, I suppose it will be OK. Sign here.'

Mario signed the docket and collected the small brown package. The man turned and called back.

'Oh yes, I nearly forgot and it's important. Tell your aunt that someone will try and get over on Monday to repair the rogue unit, the materialisation problem – it must be fixed, in fact between you and me it's against the law to operate the system as it is. The other engineer's been given a ticking off, he should have shut it down. Just keep it switched off. OK?' He winked. 'Bye.'

Mario waved politely and shut the door. They *were* easygoing, no wonder his aunt had had problems. 'Just interested in the money, probably,' he muttered to himself.

He carried the precious package carefully back into the living room and placed it on the coffee table. He stared at it, long and hard, for several minutes.

Uncle Emilio was in there!

The *legendary* Uncle Emilio.

He interlocked his fingers as he tried to fight the germ of curiosity which grew within him. What was Uncle Emilio like? The waiting and the stories combined with the prospect of an actual appearance were too much for Mario.

He would surprise his aunt.

What if, when she came home, he could have Uncle Emilio sitting in a lounge chair, smiling and wishing her '*buona sera*'? Wouldn't that be fantastic? It did not take him long to convince himself that there would be nothing wrong in preparing a special 'welcome home' for her.

He opened the brown wrapping paper and carefully removed a sheaf of foam padding. Inside this there was an envelope and a sparkling square sheet of glass. As the light hit the surface a rainbow of colours refracted from it. Somewhere within the whorl of colour there was a figure, waiting patiently to be animated.

Mario looked at the envelope. A neat, typewritten address, and below that an indication of the contents:

'Invoice – original photograph.' He paused for a moment. His first thought was to open it and take a look at the picture, but then he dismissed the idea. Aunt Edda would think he was being nosy about the cost. He would keep to his original plan.

Mario reverently blew the specks of dust which had settled on the plate and crossed over to where the control box was fixed. A wall switch threw the power on. Mario was careful to disengage the other house holograms and then double-check that only laser gun number 9 would be working.

He took a deep breath and gritted his teeth.

Then he pressed a button and fed the glass plate into the side of the box. Above him, the laser clicked into action. He trembled with excitement and anxiety, all rolled into one. He crossed back to the other side of the room and sat in the large armchair.

He waited for his Uncle Emilio to appear.

The laser gun aimed a thin shaft of light down into the room. Slowly, a vibrating, shimmering image began to form at the far end of the lounge. As the image became more solid it seemed to be dressed in a big black cloak. But when the laser had filled in the detail, it became apparent that it was in fact a large heavy overcoat.

Uncle Emilio had his head bent forward.

A dark brown fedora hat with a thick black band hid Uncle Emilio's features. Gradually the hat rose as the face turned upwards to look towards Mario.

Something was not quite right.

Perhaps the original photograph had been of poor quality, but the image did not quite seem to be as clear as Aunt Edda's other holograms. It almost seemed as if it had been drawn, or painted.

Mario sat quite, quite still.

Beneath the brim of the fedora a dark scowling face peered out. The eyes froze everything within their view.

Mario was not sure what to do. He had always

59

thought that Uncle Emilio was a happy, friendly character. This figure looked positively menacing.

'Hello, Uncle Emilio,' said Mario nervously, forcing a smile.

Uncle Emilio stared back. His lips moved but nothing could be heard.

'*Buon giorno, signor*,' said Mario, remembering that perhaps Uncle Emilio didn't speak English.

Uncle Emilio moved forward.

His face was much easier to see now. It was a close-shaven but rugged face, pock marked and with what seemed like a series of thin scars on one cheek. The eyes were dark holes set back in a hard mask. Suddenly the jaw moved in angry agitation, but no sound came out. As Uncle Emilio moved forward his arm passed through the edge of a chair.

Mario felt uncomfortable. He was not sure that he had done the right thing. He had thought that this would be a happy occasion, but now he was scared.

The spit and fizz of a faulty circuit board buzzed from the box on the wall. Uncle Emilio shimmered once more and then glowed with a certain presence which had not been there a moment earlier.

The face beneath the hat brim grinned. The hard lines and ice-cold stare warmed into a friendly, laughing smile. Everything was OK!

'*Grazie!*' said Uncle Emilio as he held his arms out wide. Mario forgot all his fears. A reciprocal grin spread across his own face. Uncle wanted him!

He ran into Uncle Emilio's welcoming arms. The

figure held him tightly, perhaps just too tightly.

The box on the wall fizzed again. A thin curl of smoke crept out from one of the ventilators.

Aunt Edda was furious that she had had to let herself in. She had been busy at the Mall and was laden down with shopping. Too many parcels occupied her arms to have to bother with finding keys. But no Mario had answered the door and in the end she had just had to struggle.

In the hallway she called out his name, but there was no reply.

Never mind, she decided, Mario was big enough to look after himself. As she stopped in the lounge for a moment to catch her breath she noticed the brown paper wrapping. She could have jumped for joy. The hologram had arrived at long last.

Her Emilio was here!

She tore open the white envelope on the coffee table to see the report on the transfer. She hoped it was A+ quality. Just below the letterhead was a supplementary note under the heading COMMENTS:

Poor image. C+.

Aunt Edda frowned as she picked up the photograph. Maybe it was a little old, but the picture was good. Her handsome Emilio stood proudly in front of the cinema, one hand twirling his fine bushy moustache. It had been a pity about the gruesome pictures and posters in the background, but they did bring back memories. They had seen the film together that night – from the projectionist's box:

L'Onorata di Famiglia – a gangster movie about a kidnapping. She shivered as she remembered the gruesome ending.

As she was about to put the photograph back in the envelope something caught her eye.

Behind Emilio was the large poster advertising the film. The main godfather of the gang, black coat and wide-brimmed fedora, glared down at Emilio from the hoarding. His outline was circled in the familiar orange ring.

'Stupid, stupid!' cried Aunt Edda, 'they have a-done the wrong man!'

In a rage of passion and disappointment she picked up a marble paperweight and threw it at the fizzing control box. Only after she had removed every hologram plate from the box and crunched them all into a thousand pieces beneath her heel did she feel better.

She would send the entire lot back for credit.

She dried her tears.

Now where was Mario? She did *so* want him to meet his Uncle Emilio before he went home.

The Card

Pete Simpson felt special again. Like a true young executive. It was so good, just knowing that it was sitting there in his wallet, snuggled comfortably against his chest, close to his heart.

The day passed in a spending spree of numbing happiness. Only the mysterious problem of the recent rash took the edge off the fun. Occasionally he would have to slip into a doorway or an alleyway to scratch himself. In Top Man's shop it had become so bad that he had dashed into a changing cubicle.

It was *not* his imagination as the doctor had suggested.

The itching was getting worse and it was especially bad on Saturdays. The problem always seemed to increase as the day wore on.

It had started when he first began to use his card in earnest. He remembered giving his Personacard to the salesperson in Down Price Records and Tapes. He had bought himself a pile of compact discs and some cassettes for his personal stereo. The card had felt soft and slippery in his hand, and while it was being processed through the voucher machine his fingers had started to prickle and sting as if he had been holding a sprig of nettles.

The light grey pallor of his skin was clearly visible now. Even Anne had noticed it. Last weekend he had visited Computer Playland. He bought a new copy of the Investment Markets computer software game. He didn't have a computer yet, but that would follow. His mouth had begun to feel dry and a sales girl had made some joke about how strange he looked. 'Like a zombie.' On his way out he had caught sight of himself in a mirror. He did look unwell, his cheeks a pitted freckly colour.

He put it down to the excitement, the new freedom. Pete had never been so excited by a credit card before. He had even taken days off work just so that he could use it more often. To be able to play with it. It seemed so much more pleasurable to use than the other cards. Store staff were friendlier, shop managers instantly took over his enquiry from their assistants, preferring to deal with him personally. Goods could even be delivered direct to his door if he so wished, there was no need to lumber around with heavy bags. The production of a Personacard revealed a hitherto unknown level of respect and courtesy.

But today his body was even hotter than usual and irritatingly prickly. He ached for a warm bath. Perhaps it was nerves.

He stood before Fashion-Guy – jewellery for the modern man. The gold bracelet he wanted was still there. Twenty-five per cent off as well. Personacard was taken.

He felt dizzy.

Perhaps it was time to return home.

He turned to go. A pain, like a hard claw, gripped his chest. His shirt felt wet. He fell against the window, drips of sweat ran off his forehead and down his nose. He was in agony.

Suddenly he cried out: 'All right, all right.'

Startled shoppers stopped in their tracks, wondering whether or not they should offer some assistance. But they passed on by.

Pain turned to pleasure as he went into the shop.

That afternoon he visited a further five shops.

As he left Nixon's at five o'clock, with his new multi-task wristwatch, he gripped the handles on his carriers more firmly and told himself that he had done enough for today.

Back at the house he caught the departure of the Habavan Delivery Service. They had dropped off all the goods purchased from one of the bigger stores. Sue was home early too and could be seen struggling to put the boxes into a neat stack inside the hallway.

He rushed up the pathway and through the door.

Amongst the mountains of cartons and bags (and a red-faced Sue), sat Anne, perched on the stairs. Her spectacles shook, her pitiful face a picture of disbelief. Empty and staring.

Pete stood in the doorway, the bags hanging from his long arms. Sue was the first to turn on him.

'There's something wrong with you, do you know that, something serious. You need help.' She pointed at the lonely figure who sat at the bottom of the stairs, '*Your* girlfriend, *my* sister, who, for reasons I can't even begin to understand, still wants you, she came round here to talk to you about these crazy spending sprees! What do we find? More of it all! Have you gone quite mad? It's never been this bad before and you look terrible!'

His chest felt tight.

He was angry. They just didn't seem capable of understanding. And mad? Not him. He was far from that, he was clever, bright, a financial wizard. Sensibly handled, credit could work *for* you.

'How did you buy all this?' asked Anne softly, looking up with a kind of desperate plea. 'It was with *that* bloody card, wasn't it? Peoplecard or whatever it's called!'

Pete felt a movement within his jacket pocket, something had shifted uncomfortably inside his wallet.

'*That bloody card!*' he said indignantly. 'This is a card that commands the attention I deserve, wherever I go.'

'Pete?' said Sue with a quizzical look. There had been a strange glint in his eye.

'*Personacard*,' Pete hissed. 'You've got to be the right person for a *Personacard*.'

'Right person? What a lot of—' but Sue never finished.

Anne stood up and replaced her spectacles.

'Give it to me, now!' she said, desperately.

'What?'

'The card, this Persona thing, give it to me now, we'll go straight upstairs and cut it in half. Maybe I can give you something to pay some of this lot off, perhaps they'll even take some of it back! We can talk to the consumer advice people, together. What do you say, start again?'

Pete felt another movement in his wallet, but this time there was also an acute itch, almost a sharp yet dull ache, which spread across the right side of his chest.

'Give it to me now, or we're through,' insisted Anne.

'No, just shove off, leave me to live my own life.'

Something next to his chest purred like a fat contented cat. It was a purr of approval.

'I want the card!' screamed Anne.

Somewhere a hackle rose.

'Hell, OK, OK! Don't worry, OK!'

Pete dropped one of the bags, his hand shot inside his coat, fingers exploring beneath his jacket. The shirt was still damp, and torn. He pulled his hand away. The fingers were wet with blood.

'Pete!' cried Sue. 'What is it, what have you done to yourself?'

He rushed past them, taking the stairs three at a time.

'Just leave me alone,' he cried back. 'Just sod off and leave me alone.'

The girls heard the crash and shudder of a slammed door at the top of the stairs. Anne looked

67

at Sue. She had no more tears left, she had cried herself dry.

'Anne,' said Sue quietly, 'who was he talking to just then?'

Pete was furious with Anne, but more so with Sue. Her being Anne's older sister didn't make life easy for him. Spies everywhere! He couldn't wait to get out of the house. So-called democratic lefty house share! There were queues every morning for the bathroom, rotas for using the kitchen, no-smoking areas, all that crap. At least he had his own room, even if it was at the top of the house.

He'd show them all soon, close some top deals, get promotion and buy a studio flat in Battersea. He knew a good broker and a good agent, personally.

The confrontation had ruined his day, and he had been unable to rest. As he lay on top of his duvet, his mind drifted back over the past few weeks, back to when he had first been introduced to the card . . .

He had never noticed the shop on the corner of Eastern Road before, which was strange considering that he passed by that same corner on his short cut most nights. It was the kind of shop that he loved, a bazaar of gizmos and gadgets.

The display was mysterious, and very, very classy. A blue neon sign buzzed the name EXECUTIVE TOYS above the window. Inside, a red velvet curtain was set behind a series of small crystal tables: display stands for system organisers, cordless telephones, calculator watches, personalised diaries and all kinds of everyday items which had been customised with gold-plated trimmings. Some of the products could be engraved with the initials of your choice, free of charge.

He pressed his nose against the glass, his attention captured by something which sat proudly in the centre. It had its own spotlight, like the featured star of a show. The product itself snuggled into a black velvet case with a catch at the front. A gold trim framed the lid.

He had always fancied getting one, and he needed cheering up (he had had another one of *those* letters from the bank that morning). There it was: a portable fold-away three-inch LCD television. £99.95, and available at this special price for a limited period, according to the ticket.

Never mind about Anne and her moaning, he wanted it.

Pete stared ahead of him as he entered the shop. He felt as if he were stepping into a cinema theatre. It was peculiarly dark.

Once inside, the automatic door thudded shut behind him.

For some reason his stomach began to flutter as though something was beating its wings inside him. There were no goods displayed within the shop. There was only a single counter at the end and a quite extraordinarily large gleaming credit card voucher processor. This looked like a work of art in itself, finished in gold with an oak base.

The decor was interesting too. Long black velvet drapes hung from the walls, collecting in folds on a deep-pile black carpet. Even the counter had been covered with carpet and another spotlight picked out the credit card machine in a silvery circular pool. Peter looked up to the ceiling, but he couldn't even be certain that there was one. It was like a starless night.

'Can I help you, sir?' asked a sudden authoritative voice.

Pete looked down, startled.

Someone stood behind the counter. He couldn't see any features at first, but then the figure moved forward out of the shadows, into the edge of the silvery pool.

The man was dressed as if he might be a butler or a high-class waiter. He wore white gloves and a dark well-cut suit with white shirt and stiff collar, beneath which snuggled a black tie secured with a gold pin. A ruby coloured gemstone, which was mounted on the pin, caught the spotlight. The cuffs, with gold links, peeped out from the sleeves of the jacket.

The face was pale, a sickly white, perhaps even powdered. The bright red lips seemed to have been stuck on as an afterthought. The hair was brushed neatly back into a Brylcreemed skull cap.

It was difficult to tell his age. He looked more like a nightclub cabaret host than a shopkeeper.

'Executive Toys for Executives, sir,' said the red lips.

Pete Simpson coughed and undid the top button of his overcoat.

'The TV, the little portable one in the window?'

'Ah yes, sir. Our Executive LCD VHF. But

70

of course, I shall have it gift-wrapped for you immediately. Will that be cash or—'

'Credit,' snapped Pete, 'credit card.'

'But of course, sir. So civilised. So clean and simple, no messy money, all those contaminated bank notes and filthy coins. I have the machine right here waiting for you. Your card please.'

Pete struggled with the fat leather bundle stuck inside his pocket. He pulled hard, it wouldn't budge. Another tug and there was an awful ripping sound as the bundle came free.

'Damn it. Sorry, I've torn my coat.'

'Fat wallet, sir,' said the man, 'all those credit cards?'

Pete pulled out his Bonuscard and placed it on the counter. The man looked at it as if it were a foreign banknote of dubious currency.

'I'm sorry, sir. We don't handle that account.'

Pete frowned. It was a major card. Not to worry. He slipped the plastic back into his card wallet and produced a replacement. His Credit Trust Card.

Again the man shook his head.

'Pardon me, sir. You do not seem to understand—'

He cleared his throat before he continued. 'Here at Executive Toys we deal only with executive accounts. We try to avoid the . . . the . . . how can I put this delicately, the more ordinary, common cards. May I enquire as to whether you have the card which most young executives carry with them these days?'

Pete stared. He shook his head.

71

The man reached beneath the counter and produced a shiny folded leaflet. A thin band of gold leaf framed the green and white striped pages.

'Here you are, sir. Personacard. Are you the right person for a Personacard? Hmmmn, we shall see, won't we, sir?'

Pete picked up the leaflet. He'd never heard of Personacard before.

'It's an application form, sir, although you don't even have to send it through the post. Simply call the number on the back, it's a free call, answer a few simple questions, tell them you collected the prospectus from us and the application will be dealt with promptly, within twelve hours. Couldn't be simpler. Let it into your life, sir. Just let it in. We shall hold the TV for you, it will await your return. Good day.'

The door hissed open. A blast of cold air and a pathway of daylight entered the shop.

Pete Simpson gulped, gathered his things together and left quickly.

Back at the house he discovered that he was the first one in. He was glad, it could be so noisy sometimes and he was in no mood for company.

The usual pile of junk mail sat on the hall table. He thought he must be on every computer mailing list in the country. Pete received catalogues full of items he would never need: stretch covers on special offer, greenhouses and patio extensions, as well as the usual stream of requests for him to subscribe to some new charge card or pension scheme.

He shuffled through the envelopes and the shrink-wrapped booklets, most of which urged him to 'open immediately' in order that he might qualify for his super free gift and entry in the raffle of the century.

He was about to shove them all into the hall-table drawer, to read through later, when he stopped at one envelope in particular. A rectangular gold stripe outlined the packet. Through the cellophane window, where his name and address appeared, he could just see the edges of a green and white stripe. He turned the envelope over, on the back was the name of the sender – Personacard.

Was there a coincidence, surely they never acted that quickly and how did they know—?

Pete hesitated for a moment. Something bothered him, but he wasn't sure what. Then, with a shrug he quickly tore open the envelope.

It contained a piece of flimsy cardboard, almost in the style of an invitation, printed with green and white stripes and gold trim. In the centre, in a computer dotted script was a message:

'Personacard, Mr Simpson, have YOU applied yet? The new card for tomorrow's world, today. Are you the right person to carry a Personacard? Let it into YOUR life, why not call us now?'

He gathered the mail together and hurried up the stairs to his attic room. Once inside, he pulled the door shut and grabbed his radio telephone.

He carefully unfolded the Personacard application leaflet with his free hand. He punched out the telephone digits on the handset with the dexterity of a computer keyboard operator, and a voice said, 'Personacard.'

The connection had been instantaneous. Lightning fast. It had caught him unawares.

A strangely seductive, synthetic drone continued:

'Personacard. Let it into your life. We're glad you called Mr Simpson.'

It had scared him. He was expected.

The questions had been simple. The fact that he carried a Bonuscard immediately reduced the rest of the enquiries to the basic address and telephone number. But Pete knew that they were only observing a formality even asking for that. After all, they knew where he lived already, didn't they? He had the invitation to prove it.

They also asked if he had had a personal introduction.

He mentioned Executive Toys.

'Your card will be with you tomorrow.'

The voice wished him a 'good day', and, 'Don't forget. Let it into your life.'

He clicked the receiver shut.

Pete remained seated, in the silence. He failed to notice the crawl of the early evening shadows which filled the attic room's maze of angled corners. In between the shadows sat dozens of electronic gadgets: there was a tie press, a digital alarm clock radio and a computer calculator which sat next to the control box for a pair of electronic scales which had somehow managed to disappear beneath the bed, next to the young executive shoe caddy and polisher.

Eventually, exhausted, he fell asleep.

The card arrived the following morning.

A smartly uniformed delivery courier stood outside the front door. He looked much the same as any other delivery courier except for one detail which Pete noticed instantly.

He wore snow-white gloves.

One of the gloves held a small brown package.

'Mr Peter Simpson?' asked a beaming face.

Pete nodded.

'For you, sir, special delivery, please sign here.'

Pete took the package and scribbled a signature in pencil on a clipboard sheet.

'Thank you, sir. Good day.'

Pete watched as the man bounded cheerfully down the steps and jumped into a green and white striped van. The courier leant out from the window as the van pulled away. 'Bye now. Remember, sir, let it into your life!'

Pete felt cold. The words were caught on the chill morning air. He shivered on the steps, feeling an icy mixture of excitement and fear.

That had been the start of it all.

Now Pete sat in his wicker chair staring out in front of him. The two girls had given up hammering on the door and had gone downstairs again. The front door had slammed.

He shivered slightly from the cold, but for some reason he didn't feel like putting a new shirt on. He had bathed the gash in his chest, it was deep but didn't require stitches. The Personacard had

75

cut right through everything, the wallet, Filofax and even his clothes. Everything. And yet it didn't seem particularly sharp.

He had pulled the card clean out of the wound, the little gold band glistening with beads of dew-drop redness. His name was raised in proud gold letters on a green and white striped background: Peter Simpson, Esq. The right person for a Personacard.

Beneath this was the embossed expiry date.

He hadn't really noticed it before.

He frowned at what it said, and gasped.

He felt a sense of panic. There must be some mistake, credit cards were usually issued for a year at least.

Pete felt well. Better than ever in fact. He had rested and felt much calmer now. The Personacard literature had been spread out on the bed. A picture of the headquarters filled the front page: a large black block of a building, windowless and featureless, but with such presence and a P.O. Box address. The design positively glowed with class. He would ring them first thing about the date on the card.

He ran his hands over his body. 'My God,' he thought, 'I've never felt so good.'

The itching no longer bothered him, in a funny sort of way it felt quite pleasant.

He would go out tonight. Up West maybe and do the clubs, have a meal and pick up some girls. Real girls who knew how to spend and how to live.

His left hand stopped at his waist. He let his

fingers stroke the side of his rib cage again. There were bumps, tiny ones like heat lumps. He looked down at his skin. It was difficult to tell with the evening attic light what was happening, but it looked darker, a kind of grey wash.

He grunted something to himself along the lines that young executives weren't wimps, and slapped himself on the chest.

He crossed the room to the dressing table and picked up his Personacard. It felt warm, alive, anything but plastic. The surface had a texture which was quite unique. He stroked the green band, he felt the stamp of his name. Then he cradled the card in his hand and squeezed it gently like a sponge.

Pete stared at his reflection in the dressing-table mirror. His eyes appeared to sink deeper into his head. Dark craters circled the green pupils as he held his own gaze.

He continued to squeeze the card, gently, gently, gently. Drops of crimson wetness gathered at the end of his clenched fist and then dripped, drop by drop on to the pine wood floor.

The earlier purring returned.

The rash now covered his body, giving a peculiarly comforting sense of well-being.

He grinned into the mirror and whispered the Personacard message:

'Let it into your life? Why not? Come in.'

Sue had become increasingly alarmed by the strange muffled cries, a confusion of pain and pleasure, she couldn't tell which. The light had been on all night

77

and Pete had got in late. Sue had called Anne, who had hurried round in case there was something seriously wrong.

The man next door had broken into the room for the girls. He wasn't sure who or what he was looking at at first, but Sue knew that it was Pete. He was stretched out on the top of the bed, eyes wide, and muttering about being the 'right sort of person', and 'you know it makes financial sense'. The girls stared in horror. Sue thought that he had covered himself in body paint, perhaps he had been out to one of his wild Yuppie parties. But the green and white stripes seemed to glow *beneath* the skin rather than on it, and the gold line which ran around his body felt cold and smooth to the touch, like real gold.

Pete whispered in the neighbour's ear as he leant over to search for a pulse:

'I let it in—'

Anne ran from the room after she touched the raised lettering which protruded from Pete Simpson's side.

It was too much to take.

It gave his name and, just beneath that, a bright shiny expiry date.

Tomorrow.

Freebies

The old one-eyed Chinaman who stood in the market place was giving them away. He wasn't giving them to quite *everyone* though. Just people who took his fancy, and who said nice things about the pile of old junk that he was selling from his stall. The old man appeared to like kids, and was acting up like some weird oriental Santa Claus.

Dad had bought a wok from him, for Mum, it was going to be a Christmas present. I'd have preferred to go to Habitat, then you knew where it'd been, but Dad wanted to be his usual 'grassroots' self and buy the thing from the people who knew, *really knew*, about woks.

Dad really can be a boring old fart sometimes.

I wasn't so sure that Mum would know what to do with the thing anyhow, or whether or not she even wanted one. Her mind would be on other things this year, it being the first one without Grannie.

So I ended up being dragged around Chinatown, in the middle of dirty smelly old Soho, on a busy

Saturday afternoon, just to get a piece of authentic Chinese frying pan!

The old Chinaman gave me the creeps. A wrinkled prune of a face, with green teeth in a gap-filled mouth, which gasped hot stale breath when he bent down to whisper in my ear.

'Please take it,' he grinned, 'for you. It is present. For you, how you call it? A freebie. With every twenty wok I sell today, a freebie. Yes, it is good, eh?'

He had to be joking, and what a coincidence.

How'd he know about my little hobby, anyhow?

It didn't matter, I'd got another one for the collection.'

I looked at the little black plastic box with the dangling chrome chain. He must have read my mind and I could certainly read Dad's. He just groaned. You see, I had a thing about 'give-aways'. Collected them all the time, out of breakfast cereal packets, from petrol stations when we got petrol, supermarkets, anywhere really.

I just liked them, like little trophies. Freebies, as the man said.

'What is it?' I asked.

'It doesn't matter,' said Dad through clenched teeth, 'it's kind of the gentleman to give us anything at all.'

'It clever key ring,' said the Chinaman, 'instructions in little panel, where battery go. Batteries not included. You like? I sell you packet, here. Special price to you of one pound ninety pence.'

A leathery hand unfolded to reveal a packet of

digital watch batteries, produced from nowhere like a card in a magician's card trick.

Dad's face twitched. I sniggered.

'Crafty old sod,' I said to myself, 'he's just got Dad to shell out on a couple of batteries that he wasn't expecting to have to buy.'

Dad gave him what he sometimes called one of his 'old-fashioned' looks and pressed two pound coins into the Chinaman's palm.

The hand closed.

The old man wished Dad a happy Christmas, and turned to serve another customer who was interested in a wok set.

We didn't even get the change.

That Chinaman was smarter than he looked.

Dad decided that we should walk to Trafalgar Square and perhaps take a bus or taxi back to Brixton. He still wanted to poke around in a few shops, just in case he saw something else he fancied.

'We've got to help Mary through Christmas now that Edith won't be with us this year. You know how dependent she was on the old bat—' he corrected himself, 'the old dear. Help her to take her mind off things, OK?'

He winked at me. I smiled back to keep him happy.

Hypocrite. I knew what he really thought about Grannie.

I hated it, too, when he called Mum Mary, so familiar, as though I was one of their wally 'drinks party' friends instead of a kid, and I could never get

81

used to Grannie being called by her first name. It wasn't right. As far as I was concerned Grannie was Grannie, and she'd always been around.

'You're growing up now, Sarah,' he'd said to me once, 'you must start to behave more like an adult. I also think it's about time you stopped playing with all those stupid gimmicky toys you litter your room with.'

He always went on and on about how we were slaves of the 'consumer society' as he called it, and how I was a mindless dingbat to go along with it all.

That was a joke coming from a middle-aged bloke who thought he was really IT.

Me? I just liked freebies, that was all.

Dad hated the fact that the old Chinese prune had given me another toy. The joke was on him though: he'd bought me the batteries to go with it!

As we walked down Charing Cross Road I turned the little plastic tag case over in my hand. I wondered at first why a key ring needed batteries, but then I realised what it was.

In gold lettering on one side was a line of Chinese letters, beneath that in English it simply said 'Chang's Quality Woks, Brewer Street, London, England (main distributors).'

On the other side of the tag it said 'Key-Finder'.

The little yellow paper stuffed inside the base explained it all in sentences my teacher wouldn't have liked:

Kee-Finder will nether let yuu down if kees yuu lose or mislay. Just whistle. If yor keys are within a

30' radios our tag will immeddiately return call with a serees of clere tones.

It was one of those lost-key locators. I was really pleased.

I couldn't wait to try it out.

Dad wanted to go into a bookshop near the National Gallery, 'Better Books'. He wanted to get Mum (or Mary) another present. I followed him in while trying to fit the pill-shaped batteries into the base of the key tag.

The shop was jam-packed. Christmas shoppers, cookery books and pictures of the Royal Family everywhere.

A lady in the shop, with glasses and a bun on the back of her hair, pinned a big round yellow badge on my coat lapel. She asked me if I liked books and wished me happy Christmas. There was a miniature book stuck in the centre of the badge, the size of a postage stamp. It opened, with pages like a real book. Above this was the message: *Better books are Better!*

It was a really good freebie, I hadn't seen one like that before.

Dad took my badge off when he saw it, and slapped it down on the counter. The lady with the bun glared at him.

Dad (or Jim if we're into parent-speak), was getting himself all worked up again. Mumbling about me being an easy target, a sucker for it all.

He bought a hi-fi magazine on the way out of the shop, and there was a freebie stuck to the cover with a bit of Sellotape. A Hi-fi Casebook pencil sharpener.

It was clever. A little plastic compact disc with the sharpener on the other side of the spindle hole. On the way home he never lifted his head out of his precious hi-fi magazine once! Typical. He's just as much of a consumer-head as everyone else!

He wouldn't let me whistle on the bus, but when we got off at Brixton Hill I tried to get the Key-Finder to work.

So I whistled. I whistled at it, whistled in it, practically took the thing apart. Nothing.

Dad got mad, which was *really* ironic considering all the fuss he'd been making about the thing, said he'd a mind to go all the way back to Soho and give the man his batteries back.

I wasn't *that* bothered. After all, it had been free, it looked pretty and I could still put my keys on it if I wanted to.

But I had another idea, another use for it.

'Are you going to chuck it?' asked Dad as we turned into our drive, past the dustbins.

I shook my head.

Dad stopped and turned on his heels. A single finger was lifted.

'I'm warning you, are you listening, young lady? You leave Dylan alone, he's got a hard enough life as it is trying to survive in the Brixton Hill gardens with all that other nonsense you've fixed on the poor little devil's collar!'

I just smiled, politely, and then shoved the key tag deep into my coat pocket. Dad could be *such* a pain.

Dylan was scratching himself on the porch mat as we walked up the path.

The front door opened, Mum (or Mary), stood in the doorway.

She didn't look good. I sighed.

Dad (or Jim), was making caustic comments in the living room about how the Christmas booze had seemed to be prematurely lowering its level. The surface line in the large bottle of Gordon's, which sat on the Habitat trolley, was certainly nearing the bottom.

Even I noticed that.

But then again, Mum was depressed.

I spent my time out in the kitchen trying to make the key tag work, but it wouldn't give out so much as a peep. Dylan had struggled into the kitchen too.

Mum and Dad were rowing again and Dylan wanted to get out of their way.

I didn't blame him.

Dad was making the usual fuss about how she had to pull herself together, she'd a family (and him) to look after, just because Edith's number had come up we didn't have to spend the entire Christmas in mourning.

Then he threatened to re-convert the Grannie flat which we'd had built next to the garden shed. He'd always threatened to make it into an outdoor aquarium.

Ah well.

And my new freebie didn't work.

Dylan purred smugly down at me from the top of the boiler. His head was lowered from the weight of his great collection of Cat Consumables. Mum called him our 'Consumer Kitty'.

I attached the key tag on to his collar along with the other freebies:

his Katto-Kipper personalised name disc

plastic Burger King bun

miniature Coca-Cola bottle

Holiday Inn room tag

MHI luggage label

Kellogg's Munchkin Man

and a Dr Who Energiser ring which wrapped around his neck.

That had been a special 'give-away' at the Arndale Shopping Centre in Croydon, he liked that best of all.

Dylan opened his sleepy eyes and stretched his paws and shook his new toy. Then, with a loud miaow, probably a 'thank you', he made for the kitchen door. His freebies crashed into the cat flap on his way out.

In the living room they were still rowing.

Dad's voice was getting really loud.

Outside came the rumble of an approaching car. I suddenly had a bad feeling.

I heard Mum's glass smash at almost the same time as we heard the screech of brakes out in the front road.

There was an awful short tangled wail. The kind of sound cats make when they scrap. Then silence.

I heard Dad yell, 'Oh my God, no!'

Dad can be *so* dramatic.

* * *

Yesterday was miserable: black and solemn.

Dad blamed me. He was really mad. But it was good of him to dig Dylan a nice neat grave out in the back garden.

He kept muttering about how there had been far too much on his collar, and how the whistling key ring had been the final straw. Just slowed him down, so when he'd run across the street he was an easy target.

Mum told him to shut up, that he'd upset 'the child'.

'The child' indeed. I just ignored her.

We put Dylan in the soft soil where Mum had planted the Hobson's Garden Centre roses, just in front of the Grannie flat.

We buried him with full honours, all his toys intact. I'd wanted the key ring back, just as a souvenir, but Mum was almost sick when Dad tried to find it. It was like picking a favourite strawberry out of a collapsed flan.

She called me a funny word. I didn't know what it meant, but I didn't like the sound of it at all.

A ghoul?

You *can* go off parents.

Sleep was very difficult that night, in fact everything was a funny blur. The air in my bedroom seemed thick and it was difficult even to breathe.

I opened the dormer window and looked down into the garden.

It was dark and cold, but winter clear outside.

A grey cloud passed over, and the grass in front

of the Grannie flat reflected moonglow once more.

The garden shone.

A newly heaped pile of top-soil marked the spot. I had scratched Dylan's name on a coke can, and fixed it in the ground, a temporary tombstone.

The TV offer peacock wind-chime which hung within the window-frame sang softly as a gentle wind got up.

A last goodnight to Dylan.

I shivered and scrambled back to bed.

I must have forgotten to close the window because I remember the sounds well. So bright. Icy sharp.

There was the rustle and flutter of feathers against branches.

A low warbling sound, and then a single hoot.

It was our owl, and he had come to speak to Dylan.

He'd startled me. Through half-closed eyes I watched as the shadows of the branches shimmered across the bedroom wall. Tangling into twisted claws.

Dylan would sit for hours on the window-ledge. The owl came often. Dad said that it was unusual to find a bird like that in Brixton.

Dylan and the owl were friends. But now he'd have to find somebody else.

I pulled the sheet up tight to my neck, eyelids heavy with sleep.

There was a high-pitched whistle outside.

The owl was preparing to fly from the tree.

It shook its feathers and then let out a strange kind of 'hoot'.

And then another . . . it was really scary.

Almost a whistle.

Just after that I heard a strangled muffled growl, far away, from deep beneath the still cold earth.

I sank and sank, down and down, into the softness of dream.

My eyes were not quite closed. Not yet. But I knew.

From the distance the owl cried out once more. I couldn't do a thing. Couldn't even move. I didn't know if I was awake or dreaming.

There was a familiar scratching on the bark of the tree outside my window. A slow and perhaps painful kind of shifting.

The shadows of branch claws trembled across the wall as something pulled itself along a main bough.

There was a shape framed within the window, dead eyes that glowed, and then the soft plop as it dropped from the sill down on to the floor.

I heard a gasp, the momentary 'puff' of the eiderdown as though something heavy had landed on the bed.

Outside the branches rustled. Twigs cracked.

I became aware of a gentle repetitious pumping at the bottom of the bed, and then a warm comforting vibration in the small of my back like an electric motor.

I was afraid. At first.

But I'm a big girl now.

Mum was very excited. 'Hysterical,' Dad said. She kept asking him over and over about the white and ginger hairs at the bottom of the bed.

He told her not to be so silly and to 'lay off the sauce'.

I think it was the blood that really bothered her. That and the soil-clogged Burger King bun she found next to the pillow.

I can understand why she was so upset, but she's all right now.

What pissed me off most was Dad, saying that I could never bring another freebie into the house again.

I'll do what I want!

Have I got a surprise for them, for Christmas!

I've been practising my whistles, and I've got lots of ideas for using those key rings now. I went to Brixton and caught the tube, all the way up to Chinatown, and all on my own too. I got a whole bunch of the tags from the old Chinese wok man.

We did a deal. I'd keep quiet about his fiddle with the batteries.

Tonight I'm going to go and see Grannie at the cemetery.

It's just up the road.

Mum misses her so, and it'll serve Dad right.

The key ring works fine now. Fine.

Best freebie I've ever had.

Baby

Pippa couldn't make up her mind about the black iron grid. Was it designed to keep people out or to keep something in? The monotonous rows of black net sheeting ended where she stood. Here, on either side, they met two shiny black metallic pillars, electronic sentinels which guarded the kingdom of Mr and Mrs Antrobus.

It would be like entering another world.

She pressed her head against the pattern of perfect squares, chubby hands clasping the grid on each side of her face.

The house was a mixture of mathematical shapes, lines and angles, and quite different from most other houses. It looked lonely and severe.

'Come on Pippa!' squealed Alison.

'All right, all right, I am. Just don't rush me.'

Alison laughed and sang a rhyme in ridicule of her friend's nervousness. Pippa removed her head from the railings and looked at her in disgust. Alison was far too big to be playing nursery games.

91

'How old are you?' she asked, looking down her nose.

'Old enough to go out with Freddy Miles to-morrow night,' crowed Alison, 'and if you don't get in there and earn a bit of the necessary we'll be going on our own, without you. That means you don't get to go out with his brother. OK!'

A vision of Kevin Miles floated into Pippa's mind and smoothed away the ripples of reservation. Everyone, but everyone, wanted to go out with him. His family had only just been allowed to leave the Mall after doing their stint for the economy, so now he was up for grabs. At last she had an opportunity. Two solid weeks' dieting in order to get in better shape had also contributed to the big day.

Pippa took a deep breath and approached the black mesh grill fixed in the right-hand pillar. She stared at the brass plate below. Her freckled reflection stared back through the engraved message:

PRESS KEY FOR INSTRUCTION
MR AND MRS ANTROBUS

Beneath this a smaller, newer plate had been added:

RESIDENTIAL – (NON-CONFORMITY PERMISSION
NO 584. HAPPY STERLING) – STRICTLY PRIVATE

'Press key for instruction?' Pippa's nose wrinkled. 'Push the door bell, dummy!'

She waited for a moment and then reached out to the square brass button, and pressed it home.

She was startled by an almost instantaneous

response. A grating, yet easy monotone sounded through the mesh; rubber bands for vocal cords.

'Antrobus residence. Appointment only. State name and business. Thankyou.'

Pippa swallowed hard. She pulled a face and looked at her friend.

'Go on, hurry up!' said Alison, 'I've got to go, it's getting dark. We agreed, we had a deal and I've seen you to the gate.'

'State name and business. Thankyou,' repeated the voice.

Pippa turned back to face the grill.

'Pippa Douglas, for Mr and Mrs Antrobus. Your reception lady's a friend of Mum's, you see. I was supposed to baby-sit for you tonight. We arranged—'

She was cut off.

'Date of birth. Place of birth. Thankyou.'

Alison giggled. Pippa frowned. What did it want to know that for? This seemed like an extraordinary procedure just to get into somebody's front garden.

'Er, 25th March 1991. King's College Medical Centre.'

'Place of birth. Don't be clever. Thankyou.'

'He means the town, dopey,' nudged Alison with a grin.

'Sorry. I wasn't thinking. London.' Then she added, 'Denmark Hill if you must know, non-Township category.'

'Cheeky thing,' said Alison. Pippa kicked her shin.

There was a moment's silence.

'Affirmative link. You are expected. Enter. Proceed directly. Thankyou.'

The iron pillars shook as the gears and pulley chains laboriously engaged and the two gates slowly swung inwards.

'What's with the dates and birth place? I don't like this,' said Pippa.

'Perhaps they can check. Make sure it's you. I dunno. Anyhow, get in there. Stop making such a fuss. You'll be well paid. He's very rich, Dad says he makes all our electronic stuff. Made our 3D video, it's a good one too. I bet it's posh inside. I'll ring you tomor—'

'Hurry up. Silly chatter. Wasting time. Thankyou,' interrupted the monotone.

The walk from the front gates to the house seemed like a mile trek. As Pippa got nearer, the enormous glass and red-brick building stretched further back from view. An occasional glance over her shoulder confirmed that she hadn't got very far. It felt as if she was approaching the house through the wrong end of a telescope.

The gates had closed behind her as soon as she had entered the garden. Did they close more quickly than they had opened?

'It wouldn't be so bad if I'd baby-sat before,' she muttered to herself.

The arrangement began to worry her. What would she have to do? But her doubts quickly faded at the thought of extra pocket credits and Kevin Miles. They could go wild on Levels 7 and 8 at the Mall.

She had arrived at the main door.

The house had been described as 'Happy Sterling architect designed' by her parents. She thought that it just looked flash.

It was certainly unlike any of the other houses that the Producer Class were allowed to live in. Interest Drive and Statement Walkway had always been for those with money. The Housing Zone was, well, the Zone. Built like bargain furniture: impressive at first but falling apart after a year or so. Pippa lived there.

Everybody wanted to know what it was like inside the Antrobus place. People travelled from all over the Township just to look at it. Cars slowed down, cameras clicked. There was even a rumour that it had won awards.

The house had been built especially for them, a 'perk' for services to the Tomorrow chain of stores. It was a two-storey house, with brown tiled roofs that met at various angles like smooth ski slopes. From the outside it was difficult to imagine where the rooms would be. Rectangles of tinted picture-window glass concealed the secrets of life inside. Pippa was about to go where the other Housing Zone kids feared to tread.

There had always been stories about the place. Mr Antrobus was seldom seen, Pippa would be one of the few to find out what he looked like. It was said that he had started out as a power station engineer working from a garden shed in Sizewell, and now he had a huge factory in the London Zone.

Pippa was jolted out of her daydream by a

low-pitched hum. Instead of opening inwards, the amber-coloured front door gracefully withdrew to one side just as she had seen in TV game shows. The rubber band voice returned but she still could not tell from where.

'Please come in. Wait inside. Nice to see you.'

'It has got manners after all,' Pippa thought to herself. She entered a small brown lobby. The door glided back into place behind her.

One of the walls in front of her slid gracefully to one side.

A small grey-haired lady with gold-rimmed spectacles stood smiling at her. Her fingers were locked together so that she looked like a mandarin.

Pippa stepped out of the lobby into a room full of beiges, creams and whites.

This was the living space.

'He's let you in, has he, dear?' said the woman. 'He likes to show off. Security conscious.' She called over her shoulder, 'Aren't you, sweetheart?' And then she laughed. Pippa did not appreciate the explanation.

'Let me take your coat. Do sit down, we're a bit late, I'm afraid, so I'll have to whisk you through everything.'

She laughed again and showed her teeth. Before Pippa realised it, her coat had been removed and she was sitting on a large lambs' wool sofa. The mandarin woman swept across the room, stopping for a few seconds to adjust a crooked shade on a table lamp. She fussed with Pippa's coat, the belt had tangled. Then, with a rapid 'Tut-tut-tut,' she disappeared through an archway at the end of the room. Pippa was dazed by events. She sat on the edge of the sofa, hugging her knees and looking around the room.

It was like something out of an expensive mail order catalogue. Everything neatly in its place, precisely located and complementing the surroundings. At home, newspapers would be everywhere, cushions and curtains unmatched, and unwashed mugs scattered all over the place.

The Antrobus room was a perfect shop window.

The thick covers of the sofa and chairs melted into the cream deep-pile carpet. The walls were draped in a velvety fabric which shimmered and whispered *sheer luxury*. The walls and ceiling were individually lit, but Pippa could see no sign of light fittings. The whole effect was extraordinary.

Five minutes ago she would have considered turning around and walking back out. Now she was simply captivated by it all.

She reached out and touched the drapes, stroking the pile with her finger tips.

'Don't touch. Very expensive. Thankyou.'

Pippa jumped. The familiar voice had suddenly cut into the silence.

'Don't be such a fuss-pot, dear,' came a reply. The woman with the permanent smile and gold-rimmed spectacles reappeared through the arch.

'I'm sorry, it's with it being late, you see. I'm Mrs Antrobus, my husband is nearly ready. We very rarely go out and I get so excited when we do. Problem is we never usually leave baby,' she laughed again, 'and, truth is, we get in such a flap just thinking about it. Leaving baby for a few hours on his own is all right usually, but we really will be a bit late tonight.'

She lowered her spectacles and bent down to face Pippa. 'I'll let you into a little secret.'

Then she whispered, 'In fact you're our first baby-sitter. We've not had baby long. We've never cared for children really, so messy, so inconvenient. Our baby is different, of course.'

'Of course,' agreed Pippa, trying to hide a grin.

Mrs Antrobus giggled with delight at sharing the secret. She bounced backwards and disappeared through the archway once again.

Pippa watched her leave. She had heard that the rich could be eccentric. She was puzzled to hear that the Antrobuses never went out and that she was their first baby-sitter. It must be a very young baby, she concluded. She hoped she could handle it.

Through the archway came a short, irritable exchange. Pippa recognised the voice of Mrs Antrobus. She sounded agitated and flustered. A man's voice stabbed back with a low hiss. 'I don't know— He can be awkward, and the girl, well she's very young— Is it fair, the others were older?'

Were they reconsidering giving her the job? And *others*? She thought she was the first. The extra credits and Kevin Miles started to fade before her eyes.

She spoke up. 'Excuse me. Do forgive me, I couldn't help hearing. I'm very good with children, you've nothing to worry about.'

Mrs Antrobus reappeared.

'I'm sure you are, love. Don't mind hubby, he's such an old fogey.'

She was joined by 'hubby'.

Pippa's jaw fell.

She was expecting to see a large, distinguished, pin-striped figure, perhaps with greying hair at the temples. This should be the owner of Antrobus Electronics. Instead, a small white-haired figure crept timidly into the light. He was older than his wife, with a worn, worried face and round granny glasses.

'He's all we've got. And so demanding sometimes,' he explained.

Mrs Antrobus interrupted:

'I'll show the young lady where things are. You go and get the car out. Go on. We're *very* late.'

With that she shooed him away with her hands as if he were an unwanted animal.

'I'll prepare. Which garage? Suggest the Westland Volvo.'

The voice was all around them.

Mr Antrobus looked up, his eyes glowed. There was something of pride in them.

'Why, thank you. I think you're right. We'll take the silver.'

'Red Westland Volvo nicer.'

Mr Antrobus froze. He caught his wife's eye. His lip quivered for a moment and then broke into a wide smile.

'Why yes, of course. Thank you. How silly of me.'

'He's usually right,' said Mrs Antrobus, 'and he usually gets his own way.'

Pippa frowned. 'He' was obviously some central control device which ran the house. It wasn't surprising, considering Mr Antrobus' line of business.

Mr Antrobus caught Pippa's expression.

'Oh, he runs the entire shooting match,' he said proudly. 'Anything you want, just ask.'

'He can be such a prankster sometimes!' Mrs Antrobus broke into a girlish laugh once more.

At first Pippa was glad that the Antrobuses had gone. She had felt very uncomfortable with them. Her mum would have said she was being neurotic. But the house seemed very lonely now. What Pippa had thought was a snug, luxurious living space now appeared cold and unfriendly.

The Antrobuses' idea of the duties of a baby-sitter were rather different from what she expected. 'Just be in the house,' had been the instruction, '*just in case!* Don't worry about anything, look in later to see if he's comfy in his cot. He's so clean, so undemanding. Not like other babies at all.'

She didn't think baby-sitting would be that easy.

Before leaving, Mrs Antrobus had taken her upstairs to check that baby was all right. The nursery was to the left at the top of the stairs. Pippa had only caught a fleeting glimpse of the child. Pink and small and wrapped in smooth satin. Then Pippa had been whisked downstairs again before she could take a closer look.

Mrs Antrobus had obviously been in a hurry.

All babies seemed the same to Pippa. This one sucked its thumb contentedly.

'No bottle, no feed?' Pippa had asked.

'He'll take care of that himself.'

Pippa was puzzled.

The invitation to 'make herself at home' had included being rushed into the kitchen, shown the bathroom, and then with a 'Bye bye baby,' the couple had vanished into the late evening.

Pippa couldn't understand it.

There had been very little introduction to the child, no proper instructions except a phone number to ring 'in case of emergencies'.

They had seemed too old to have a baby, there were no toys anywhere downstairs. But then again, the entire house looked unlived in, and one did hear of older couples having children. There were lots of them on the American soaps. Pippa felt better when she remembered that Ellen Roberts in *Los Angeles Story* was probably about fifty and in the last episode her millionaire husband was on his deathbed right next door to the new baby's cot.

Pippa wondered whether or not to look in on the child again. She decided to creep up later. In any case she wouldn't really know what to do if it were to start to cry. She thought she'd freshen up in the bathroom and then watch TV.

The guest bathroom was just off the reception part of the living space. Most of the house was an open-plan design, but where there were doors an intriguing violet light control would slide them open at the pass of a hand.

101

The bathroom was the largest Pippa had ever seen. The bath was a clear plastic bubble sunk into the floor, the carpet had pile which seemed to swallow your feet. The walls were deep blue, with random whorls of scattered gold. The ceiling was spotted with tiny lights which twinkled like stars.

She looked at the washbasin for several minutes. Something was missing. A single spout hung above the basin, but there was nothing with which to turn the water on. No taps!

At first Pippa thought that this was rather funny, but after a few minutes of searching she felt mildly irritated.

'Stupid thing,' she said.

A low drone filled the air. The control centre was about to speak, but the announcing signal died away, and it said nothing.

Pippa gave up looking for the taps and decided to return to the living space. As she turned to leave, her eye caught a bright gold square in the carpet which she hadn't noticed before. It was like a platform and it had emerged out of the carpet pile. Timidly she put one foot on to the surface, and then another.

The drone returned, and then a voice.

'Seven stone eight pounds.'

Pippa turned purple with indignation.

'Never!'

'Seven stone eight pounds,' the voice repeated.

'Listen, you lying heap of micro scrap, I'm seven stone dead.'

'Seven stone eight pounds,' it repeated. 'Antrobus products accurate. Always.'

Pippa fumed. The control centre had touched upon a delicate area.

'I am not seven stone eight pounds. Something's wrong with your chips!'

'Seven stone eight pounds. No error. Overweight.'

'You're wrong!' screamed Pippa. 'I bet you were made in Taiwan!'

There was a terrible silence. Something unmentionable had been said.

The voice returned, more loudly this time.

'Very sorry. Error computed. Correct weight . . . seven stone twelve pounds.'

Pippa stamped on the platform, muttering about microchips, wires and other electronic components and what they could all do. She passed her hand before the door light and stormed out of the bathroom. As the door closed behind her the control centre spoke again.

'All right. Will confirm. You are seven stone—' it paused, '—dead.'

It hadn't said a word since their argument in the bathroom. Pippa looked around the room, searching for some kind of home entertainment. She finally plucked up courage to make a request.

'Hello there, I want entertaining.'

'Does not compute. Be precise,' came the austere reply.

'Well, tell me a joke then!'

There was an icy silence.

She paused for a moment, considering what to ask for.

103

'Is there a television?'

'Confirm TV addiction-free registration number.'

Pippa rolled her eyes upwards, it *was* being particular.

'PIP090. OK!! I'm off serious TV – I'm cured, all right?'

The voice didn't answer. Instead, a low whirring came from the far end of the room as a white wooden cabinet suddenly revolved into the floor like a vanishing Demon King. Seconds later it reappeared with a large white globe of plastic. Pippa was reminded of a huge eyeball, particularly when the globe parted in the centre like two blinking eyelids.

A beige screen was revealed. It crackled into life. Gun shots filled the air as two New York policemen chased across the Manhattan skyline. *Precinct 77*. It was a favourite 'oldie' programme, but too loud.

'Hey, how do I turn it down?' Pippa started to get up.

'Stay. My job. Thankyou.' And the volume lowered.

Pippa smiled to herself. She felt excited and had forgotten the oddity of the Antrobus couple. She even forgave the misreading of her weight. This was luxury.

She was just settling down to follow the escapades of Sergeant Weitzberg and his partner, when her blue uniformed heroes suddenly vanished. In their place a chequered grid curved into a world viewed from space. This unfolded into a bright yellow 3D title:

Microchip World.

Synthesised disco music leapt into the room. Pippa sat upright.

'It's changed channel,' she said to herself, 'I was watching *Precinct 77*.'

The volume increased. It would wake the baby.

'Turn it down. Change the channel back, please.'

On the screen an arrow pointed to a blown-up diagram of a circuit. The control centre remained silent.

'You there!' cried Pippa. 'Turn it off!'

'Eight o'clock. Saturday night. *Microchip World*. Better programme. *Precinct 77* rubbish.'

Pippa jumped to her feet and approached the TV screen. She peered around the globe to see if there were manual controls, remembering that the TV at home had both a remote control and buttons.

'Please leave. Good programme. Regularly viewed.'

This was unsettling. The control was supposed to do what she wanted. Not argue with her.

Pippa noticed a small indented panel at the top of the screen. She slid her finger-nail into the thin gap and tried to pull the panel open.

'Please leave. Preferred programme. Must watch.'

Her nail caught on something. Pippa felt a stinging sensation as a red drop crept along her finger. She pulled her hand sharply away.

'Damn thing!' she cursed. 'There's got to be a way—'

The panel flipped open to reveal a row of buttons. Licking her finger she reached back into the panel to push a single illuminated button.

Her hand rested there for a moment.

With a swift smooth action the huge white lids of the globe snapped shut. There was a crunch. The shutters cracked and splintered, slivers of plastic pierced her hand.

A sharp pain pounded up into her arm. The red drop grew to a sticky wash which dripped from her finger tips, spoiling the immaculate white rug.

The control centre had gone very quiet.

Pippa stood in the kitchen staring at the white marble wall tiles. The incident with the television played over and over again in her mind. Had the control snapped the globe shut on purpose or was it her own fault for interfering manually with the controls?

'Servants' were supposed to serve. If it had been the control's fault then it would either have been a malicious act of pique, or there was something wrong with it. For a pile of microchips and wires it had a very nasty streak. Perhaps it was programmed with 'alternative' humour? What worried her most was how to explain to the Antrobuses that there was blood on their carpet and a cracked TV case.

But how could an electronic machine be piqued or stamp its foot? It always spoke with an easy consistent voice. Too easy and consistent. Nothing was ever stressed, and yet there was marked aggression in its voice, it seemed to resent her being there.

She hoped that the Antrobuses would not be too long. What if the control centre harmed the baby just as it had harmed her?

Pippa had gone to the kitchen to run cold water

over her hand. A gold spout arched into the bowl, but once again she could not find any taps. With a deep breath she decided to ask, as a spark of courage returned.

'Where are the taps?'

'None exist.'

'How do I get water, please?' she asked politely.

Suddenly, water shot through the spout, gushing into the bowl, splashing back on to the white tiles. She remembered Mrs Antrobus's instructions, the control centre did everything.

'Too fast, please turn it down,' she said.

The flow dropped to a tiny trickle. With a sigh she held her hand under the spout. Eventually the stains dissolved and swam around the bowl to be swirled away into the waste disposal. The water was very cold indeed. This was ridiculous.

'OK, let's have it a bit faster, and hotter.'

A sound like distant thunder grew from beneath the sink. The pipes shook. An angry gurgle came nearer and nearer. The spout shuddered violently as a hard jet of boiling water exploded down on to Pippa's hand.

She cried out. Water sprayed upwards. Clouds of steam rose out of the sink. Pippa fell back against the kitchen unit, hitting her back on the edge of the work-top.

This was war.

Thinking quickly, she grabbed a tea towel and wrapped it around her red and angry hand. Tears trickled down her cheeks. She shook with a mixture of rage and fear.

The rumbling beneath the sink continued, the pipes rattled out a cacophony of sound, filling the kitchen like an expanding bubble, louder. Louder.

The bubble burst.

She heard the sound of ripping metal as the spout wrenched itself from its sink base. It shot upwards, like a model missile, nearly hitting Pippa's head. A rush of water followed, spraying high into the air and crashing against the ceiling.

Pippa screamed. She staggered out of the kitchen, groping her way through to the living space where she fell on the sofa. She buried her face in the cushions. The white eyeball with its damaged lids blinked open.

Microchip World came on the screen, the picture fuzzing occasionally into a shower of snow.

Pippa's fingers dug into the lambs' wool sofa cover.

The disco theme of *Microchip World* rolled on. The picture flickered upwards with ever-increasing speed.

An ugly 'craaaack' cut across the disco beat. The screen flashed with blue light before shattering into a grey fog. Sparks and flames flew from the rear of the TV as the screen finally exploded into the room, glass falling like snow on to the carpet.

The living area became a kaleidoscope of fireworks. Pops and crashes echoed throughout the house, concealed light bulbs were revealed as they exploded around her. Electricity pumped and pushed, force fed, around the ring-main circuit. Sparks flickered from electrical sockets which melted like soft cheese and then glowed a threatening amber.

Pippa cowered on the sofa. The house was plunged into semi-darkness. There was silence.

She would have to get out. The control centre had gone berserk. Then Pippa remembered. The reason she was there in the first place.

The baby.

Pippa sat in silence for some time, afraid to move and afraid to ask the control centre for anything further. She stared across at the staircase, worrying about the nursery above, worrying about the baby and desperately trying to summon enough courage to creep upstairs and get the child.

Was it all right? For all the noise downstairs she had heard no crying.

Perhaps the baby was dead?

The house had been silent now for a while. The glow of the ultraviolet door openers diffused a strange light around the walls and ceiling. The room was a dark cave of hi-tech.

Pippa could not risk waiting for the return of the parents and she knew it was no use calling the emergency phone number.

The control was the telephone operator.

She would have to do it. Snatch the baby and get out. Slowly, and cautiously, she slipped off the sofa. Her ears strained for the sound of the malevolent rubber band voice. The stairs were near the front door.

She felt her way upwards by sliding her good

hand slowly along the white rubber hand rail. Violet shadows lit the way to the upper passage and the nursery doorway, spilling over and down into the stairwell.

Her heart pounded in her ears. So far so good. Perhaps the control had burnt itself out, self-destructing in its rage and temper. She wondered for a moment whether or not it could see her. Did it know where she was?

She reached the top of the stairs. The stairwell opened into a passage which stretched to both right and left.

The nursery was to the immediate left.

A fluffy pink rabbit lay on the landing in front of the red door of the nursery.

Pippa edged her way along. A large coloured cartoon transfer of the Mad Hatter from *Alice's Adventures in Wonderland* had been stuck on the lower panel of the door.

Pippa passed her hand in front of the ultraviolet lamp of the door opener as Mrs Antrobus had shown her and as the door slid smoothly open the Mad Hatter disappeared.

Pippa went in.

She looked around this time. The decor was strikingly different from the rest of the house, more conventionally that of a child's nursery. Brightly coloured wallpaper depicted further characters and scenes from *Alice in Wonderland*. To the left a large cartoon of the Queen of Hearts looked down at her, whilst the Queen of Spades glared disapprovingly from the far wall.

A grinning Cheshire Cat sat half-way up the facing wall, guarding the lavishly curtained cot below.

It was impossible to see into the cot itself. Folds of net and lace swept around it to meet at a point above. The nets hung from the ceiling by a thread, creating a screen. A red light shone from beyond the nets, a child's night light? Pippa approached the cot, quietly humming a lullaby which her mother used to sing to her when she was very young.

'Hush little baby, don't you cry—'

Slowly, her hand parted the first layer of net curtain. She looked in.

The child lay quietly in the cot. Pink and warm. Instead of his thumb, a dummy now protruded from his mouth.

For a moment Pippa forgot the violence of the control, and nearly decided to go back downstairs and sit tight for the return of the Antrobuses.

'Come on then. Hush little baby. There's nothing to be afraid of, we're just going for a little walk,' she said softly.

She stooped down to cradle the baby into her arms.

How did you hold a baby?

All of a sudden she stepped on a squeaky rubber toy pig lying beneath the cot. Her heart thumped hard.

The startled eyes of the child opened wide. Bright, baby blue.

They looked right through her. The child did not cry. The dummy seemed to sit awkwardly in his mouth.

Pippa reached in and removed it. The baby smiled. An alarm wailed!

A flash of white light and a shimmer of sparks shot up into Pippa's face. The end of the dummy was a three-inch co-axial jack plug.

The image of the baby, through which her hand had passed, flickered momentarily.

A cry gagged at the back of her throat. With the 3D projection now unplugged she received a clearer view of 'the child'.

A long grey box lay under the soft satin eiderdown. Flashing digital numbers winked at her, mockingly. A thick projection lens sat centrally. Beside this a row of push-buttons and switches were set above an ever-changing pattern of red, green and blue lights which cast a random mosaic of colour on Pippa's face.

Half dazed, she read some letters on a manufacturer's plate in the top left-hand corner:

'VIDEO 3D BABY LTD. NO WORRY, NO MESS.'

The nursery door slid shut with a thud. Pippa's head swam as the monotone voice sang out from both the cradle and the room, competing with the alarm.

The baby's lips seemed to twitch and then twisted into rapid movement. Open and shut, open and shut, like a dying fish. They moved slightly out of sync with the voice which echoed around the nursery.

'You woke me up, you woke me up. Rock me back to sleep. Thank you. Stone. Dead.'

Then there was a laugh, a grotesque, crooked laugh.

'I'm a big boy now. Baby-sitter redundant item. Time for baby's feed. Video babies are clean and fun. Clean and fun. Clean and fun.'

Pippa's eyes widened suddenly as the child's mouth grew into a huge black circle.

'There'll be no mess,' it said.

The alarm stopped.

TV/OD

The feather-light new polystrone fibre sheets of Tom's bed formed the perfect tent. They almost floated on air, creating a private chamber within his bedroom. The inner sanctum for secret viewing. It just took a little rearranging, that was all. Just a little simple ingenuity.

The earpiece fitted neatly into his right ear. He could have gone stereo, or quadraphonic or even binaural if he wanted to, the Antrobus 3D/VDU was quite capable of it. It could do anything.

It was the very latest in TV sets. The result of two months' begging, borrowing and stealing.

At the moment he was on mono mode. He did have to keep one ear free for the parents, having been caught out that way the last time.

But it was quite late now. The light from the upstairs landing which normally squeezed its telltale signal underneath the bedroom door had long since gone out. He peeked from the sheets once more, just to make quite quite certain that there was no chance that he might be disturbed. The black-framed edge of the door reassured. The lights from Happy Comfort Mall twinkled through the skylight roof, the occasional security tractor beam throwing its golden hologram glow across the room. The heaped shadow from the bedclothes was thrown across the doorway.

It was safe. Everyone had gone to bed. He could switch on.

Inside his inner sanctum, his hands trembled with the anticipation of several hours of uninterrupted night viewing. Since the TV had been banned from the house he could no longer plan what he could watch. But it didn't matter. He never really planned anyway. He always *said* that he was selective but that wasn't really true. Tom would watch anything, anything at all.

Game shows, chat shows, TV advertisements, soap operas, old movies, phone-ins.

His infra-red 'remote' gently clicked on the ultra-violet cathode colour which he had placed, reverently, at the end of his bed, between his feet. Beads of sweat collected on his forehead. The excitement was just too much. The chunky ten-inch altar lit the cavern of bedclothes.

It was a game show: *Possessions*, hosted by TV celebrity Bob Bentine!

Tom was in seventh heaven.

The parents stared at him across the breakfast table. Tom was shovelling cereal into his mouth like an automaton. Shadowed eyes stared down at his bowl.

'Didn't you sleep, dear?' asked the mother parent.

'You look tired,' said the father parent.

Tom looked at them and began to sing a short catchy melody:

'If you have problems with your sleep,
Take Doze-ipan to send you deep,
Into the fairy land of dream
Where all is nice and—'

'Tommy!' yelled the mother. 'Stop that!'

She stood up from the table. Father leant forward and gently removed the spoon from Tom's hand.

Tom smiled.

'It's just a commercial,' he beamed, 'just a jingle.'

'Come on, you'll be late for school. I'll take you over to the auto-chute. The mother and I are scheduled for three hours' consumer shopping service at the Mall this morning. You'll have the Company knocking on the door!'

Without a word, but wearing a special look on his face, Tom got up and ran upstairs.

Above them the parents could hear the discordant mumble of a famous game show jingle. It spilled out from Tom's room and drifted down the stairs:

'We have no worries,
There is no recession,
Just spot the clues to gain your possessions!'

The mother's lower lip trembled, slightly.

'You don't think—'

'No,' said the father, 'we sent it back. He had counselling. No way. He listens to the Talking Book in the evenings, or plays Robot Ball with the other kids at the Club. No, everything's all right. Don't you worry now. Everything's all right.'

It had been difficult to get upstairs to bed just that little bit earlier that night. The parents had been suspicious, or so he thought. He had sat for what seemed like an eternity on the living area sofa, listening to another boring Talking Book. The tinny spatter of tiny talk leaked out into the evening. He wasn't listening. Occasionally his eyes would shift restlessly to the corner of the room, to the space where it had once stood.

A dust and grime mark outlined the spot where the cabinet had been. The cable connector was coiled carelessly behind the curtain. The plug was still cracked and hanging from a single bracket, where the father had pulled it out in a sudden rage that night.

'Why don't they send me to bed?' The question occupied his mind, willing the parents to say something.

Finally, the mother chirped up, to break the monotony:

'Come on now. Off to bed. The Digi-Time is about to bleep twenty-two hundred hours. That's late enough for a growing fourteen year old!'

Salvation!

His heart swelled. Its beat echoed in his ears. He had been about to burst. Without a second's thought he ripped off the ear-plugs and made for the stairs.

From above the living area came the bounce of another jingle:

'Time for bed, time for bed,
To float down stream and lay your head,
Relax and soothe away the day,
Take Chocolate Milk and—'
'Tommy!!' yelled the mother.

The colours from the twenty-four-gun tube shone off his cheeks. Large bloodshot eyes watched in wonder. Down and down into the tunnel of bed sheets. He surfaced for a moment to check that the door was still shut tight and that no crack of light was trying to steal into his room.

All was safe. All was secure. He returned to the inner sanctum.

The nightly game show had been interrupted. A dance of zigzag lines now fizzed across the screen.

Then there was blackness.

Anxiety flooded him. The blood drained from his face. If the set was broken he was in dead trouble, how would he get through the night without some viewing?

The blackness only lasted for a second or two. Then, from the centre of the screen a small point of light began to grow. It shuddered for a second and then twisted and writhed like a wriggling worm, as if trying to climb right out of the screen and on to the sheets.

It was Bob Bentine! Mr Show Business!

The man had perfectly matched white teeth, geometrically precise incisors. A black gloss of shiny smooth hair and a neatly trimmed goatee beard. His

119

blue eyes twinkled out from the screen, the deepest blue of the deepest ocean.

Tom was puzzled.

The background to Bob, the rest of the screen, was deep velvet night.

'Hi there! Now listen, listen carefully. Plug your ear-phones in just that bit more securely, we don't have long.'

Tom adjusted his ear-piece.

'OK, good. This message is just for you. For you alone, for all those kids out there who may be watching some TV, shall we say—illicitly!'

He laughed. The teeth flashed. Nostrils flared.

'We know that you're probably all watching alone. Perhaps a few of you are in groups, in cellars. Perhaps even in the backs of cars! It doesn't matter where, I know you're with me! We're going to make the TV experience just that bit more Exciting. That's with a capital E. EXCITING! Take this toll-free telephone number. Take it NOW, OK? 0800 666 999. The first three hundred calls will be sent free, yes you've got it, FREE, a Bob Bentine aural enhancer for your TV set. Now you can get Bob Bentine and all your other favourite TV shows right there inside your head! OK!! And it really is FREE! Call NOW, the lines are open! NOOOOWWW, back to the show!'

Tom wrestled with the sheets as his hand shot out to the bedside table. He snapped on his night light and grabbed a pencil. He frantically scribbled on the back of a *Video* magazine:

'0800 666 999.'

In the corner of his bedroom the red LED of his phone blinked beckoningly at him. He would have to be quick, and be very quiet. But it was free! And promised better, clearer television!

It arrived fast.

Super-fast via the Express Courier service.

'Private and Confidential' had been stamped all over the package. Tom was lucky enough to have answered the door when the driver had delivered it, otherwise the parents would have been nosing around again. It was a small box which slipped easily inside his pocket.

'Wrong house and wrong zone,' had been his reply to the mother when she had enquired who had been at the door.

Then there was the usual farce that evening, of having to pretend to be occupied when all he really wanted to do was to get upstairs for the night shift dose of cathode tube.

But it was worth waiting for.

This time it would be with aural enhancement.

Finally the Digi-Time beeped out twenty-two hundred hours.

'That boy's up to something,' said the father, 'he's especially keen to get to bed these days.'

'Give him time,' replied the mother, 'he's having to re-adjust to the loss of the—' she paused, even mentioning it didn't come easily after all the problems they had had with TV abuse. She gulped, '—the set.'

The father looked at her, then he raised his eyes

to the ceiling as the thump of Tom preparing for bed echoed down the stairs.

> 'Bob Bentine, Bob Bentine, it's Bobbie's hour
> of fun,
> Your heart's desires are prizes,
> With fun for everyone—'

'Tommy!'

It had been worth every agonising minute of waiting for bed.

Celebrity Memories just filled the space inside his head. Chat show hostess Gloria Gorguzz cooed and whispered from one ear to the other and then tickled him right at the back of his mind.

The aural enhancer really worked: two very tiny plug-in devices which snapped into place on the ear-plugs.

Stereo sound was good. Quadraphonic was sensational. Binaural just floated through you.

But the Bob Bentine aural enhancer simply tunnelled through to the next dimension. It was sound so real that you could almost smell it.

Touch it. Feel it. Breathe it.

Tom's hands gripped his knees. The 'Airmen' after-shave advertisement, with the souped-up Ford, had the screech of car tyres burning rubber on the bed clothes.

He was mesmerised.

Suddenly the twang of synthesiser music announced the nightly game show *Possessions*, featuring celebrity Bob Bentine. The voice inside his head announced that the show had been brought to him by the

Tomorrow chain of stores, subsidiary of Consumer Comfort Shopping Mall.

(Are you doing your bit? Keep on shopping!)

Then there was nothing. A thick treacly darkness reached out from the screen. The small wriggling figure, like a grub emerging slowly from the centre of a bad apple, crawled out.

This time the voice of Bob Bentine was inside Tom's head, crawling through his veins, rippling beneath his flesh.

'Hi there kids, it's Bobbie. I guess you've all got those aural enhancers now, and I guess there's none of the grown-ups about, huh? OK now, let's get on with this show. Get this number—'

Tom's arm shot out for his pencil.

'Rightee-oh. Toll-free number coming up, and . . . yes, you've guessed it, FREE!!! Get it down quick, you know the score: 0800 666 998. Lines are open now, and this time it's a free screen rectifier. Easy to wear, easy to use. You've got a 3D TV. OK. You've seen nothing yet. We're waiting for your call!'

The eyes sparkled. A touch of gold in a front tooth caught the light. There was a gel of swirling colour.

It was back to the show.

The smooth skin of the cathode tube reached out. The set expanded and contracted with the sound of his own breathing. The *Krunchie Krackle* breakfast cereal poured out from the screen filling his bed with delicious golden honey wheat. He reached out to touch it, but of course it wasn't there.

But, in his mind, it was.

Tom no longer viewed beneath the sheets. In brazen defiance the ten-inch TV was perched on top of the bed. He sat cross-legged on his pillow, the aural enhancer firmly in place within both ears, the strange screen rectifier goggles on the bridge of his nose.

Suddenly the screen shimmered into darkness. Here was Mr Show Business once more.

The goatee beard stabbed out at Tom.

'OK, you kids. No messing tonight, alrightee. Get this quick. Toll-free: 0800 666 997. But you've gotta pay this time. OK. The other stuff, they were freebies, getting you ready for the big one, and here it comes. You can see what our products can do, but kids – you ain't seen nothing. Not yet!'

The teeth gritted hard. The eyes filled the screen.

'It's the ultimate. We take credit discs, we take charge cards, we take anything. You've tasted real television, yeah? Now. Live and breathe it. Be it. Become your TV set. Mainline it. Remember 0800 666 997. We're awaiting your call.' A heavy laugh followed.

Tom's heartbeat quickened. He'd forgotten to get his pencil, to write the number down. Panic overtook him as he muttered the number back to himself. His shaking hand searched for a scrap of paper and a pencil. He repeated the number to himself feverishly, over and over and over and over again.

Tom nibbled the edges of his toast, working his way round the square first before commencing on the centre. Through the congealed marmalade and butter he hummed the theme tune to *Saturday Sell*. Across the table the mother watched anxiously as the edges of toast disappeared.

The rings around Tom's eyes were darker, pushing them further back into their sockets.

The father called in from the hall.

'Dorothy, Tommy! My credit disc has gone missing. Have you seen it?'

The father's face appeared behind the door, one hand deep into a raincoat pocket.

Tom stopped nibbling at his toast.

'No,' he said quietly.

The mother looked over at the father. He caught her eye.

'Are you all right, lad?' he asked softly.

Tom began to sing:

'Feeling down and out of salts and life's a total drag?

Take Feelee-fine in tablet form—'

'Tommy,' said the mother gently, 'what's the matter?'

The reception tone bleeped. There was someone at the door. A parcel for Tom.

'Excuse me, Mum, I've got to go, that bleep, well it's for me,

I've had my breakfast, shan't be late, be back at five for tea!'

He leapt from the breakfast table.

Tom sat in his usual position. Cross-legged in front of the television with the ear-plugs securely in place. The goggles were strapped to his forehead,

125

not pulled in front of his eyes. The contents of the specially delivered parcel were laid out in front of him on the bed. He didn't understand what they were, or how to use them. There was just a slip of yellow paper in an envelope:

Tonight. Channel Cable 33. 01.00 hours.

The Digi-Time showed 00.59 and 57 seconds.

The theme tune for *Possessions* twanged into his ears, rippling down his spine and curling its infectious beat around and about him. The familiar bud of Bob Bentine flowered from the central spot in the cathode tube. His mouth filled the screen.

'Hi there kids. Itzzzzzz Bobbie!! OK. Keep the screen rectifier goggles off for a moment. I hope you've got everything in front of you? Yeah! You lucky people!'

His laugh circled Tom's head.

'OK now. For REAL TV. The hard stuff. Serious viewing. In front of you are two ribbed tubes with two small black velvet pads on the ends. Yes? You've got them? OK now, here's what I want you to do. Tie those pads around your arms. Do that now.'

A swish of a drum machine pulsed through the ear-phones. A picture of a kid with the pads already attached flashed up on the screen.

Quickly Tom attached the velvet pieces.

Bob Bentine returned.

'Now. At the other end of these ribbed tubes there are two co-axial plugs. Now make sure that the digital number on the top side of each plug is set for this cable station, remember that's—'

126

'Cable 33, wild and free,
Cable 33, why that's for me,
Cable 33, for the family!!'
The station anthem burst into the room.
Bob Bentine flashed back into view.
'That's rightee. Cable 33. Now, are you with me?
The ultimate awaits you. On the rear of your set
you'll find two dipole extra cable connectors. Just
take a look now.'

Tom scrambled to the end of his bed and looked
at the rear panel. It was easy. There they were, just
beneath the main cable socket.

'OK kids. Plug in and tune in. Real cable,
real cable.'

Hands shaking, Tom pushed the jack-plugs firmly
home. Almost instantly the soothing gentle pulse of
pure television coursed into his arms.

'Does that feel good or does that feel good?
Yeaahhhh. OK, see through the rectifier. You're
gonna fly. You'll see our show tonight, that's *Possessions* for our non-regular viewers, like you've never
seen it before!! Are you ready? OK, LET'S GO!!'

Tom pulled down the goggles.

The screen melted into oneness with all things.
He *became* the game show. His mind and that of
all Cable Television in the known unreality became
a single pulse.

The secrets of the cathode tube universe were
revealed to him.

The parents waited at the Clinic's reception desk.
Behind the nurse a row of neat black letters told new

127

patients to 'Register First Please. Consumer Comfort Special Care Clinic.'

'You're very wise to have gone private,' said the nurse, 'but there's no need to worry. We'll have him shipshape very soon. The Clinic Director will be out to see you any moment now. We've got a lot of kids just like him here. It can be treated, of course. Quite simply Tommy's taken an overdose. Easily done, but I'm afraid your boy has taken the hard stuff right through the arms. Mainlining the tube. Nasty, nasty. We don't want him becoming a registered Vidiot do we?'

The mother's anxious eyes searched for sympathy in the nurse's matter-of-fact manner.

'We've always had trouble with him and television. We got rid of it, our doctor's suggestion. Just watched it all the time, he was becoming a vegetable. He still keeps singing those awful TV jingles . . . they're so corny . . . so awful—'

Tears formed drops in the corners of her eyes.

Tom stared in front of him, seeing only the bright lights of game shows and soap opera serials:

'We have no worries,
There is no recession,
Just spot the clues to gain your possessions—'

'Why hi there Tommy, you're humming the tune to my favourite game show,' said a voice.

'This is the doctor,' said the nurse, 'our Clinic Director.'

She smiled for the first time.

Tom looked up.

A figure in a white coat patted him on the back.

128

Bright ocean blue eyes looked down.
Perfectly white, geometrically precise teeth smiled.
Smartly glossed jet black hair.
Neat goatee beard . . .
Tom changed channel.

Road Food

At the sixth minute/mile point, Speedy engaged manual overdrive option 3 and pulled back on the steering column. Real speed was coming up!

The Ford glided down the freeway, down between the dark twinned pustules of Hillock 4B and 4C Delta.

A throaty growl shook the Ford for a second or two.

He was away!

The overdrive thrust pack responded well, without hesitation. Speedy was delighted. It really worked and there were none of the usual re-confirmation delays which had previously slowed down response. So what if the adjustment was illegal – this motor really shifted now!

The bonnet rose slightly, straining at the leash like a huge hound, panting and pulling; a wild hawk, ready to fly, to soar.

The second thrust pack 'cleared its throat' and moved into engaged mode. The car lurched skywards. Speedy doubted whether the wheels were still in contact with the road, and he cared even less.

It was at that point that his take-away barbecue leapt from the polymastic container.

The first effect of G-force pushed Speedy back against the seat. The second effect spread the sauce around the inside of the car. The take-away seemed to have a life of its own, covering the fur-trimmed dashboard, windscreen, nodding dog mascot, furry dice, seat covers and . . . Speedy. Speedy Sanders: *the* freeway rodder. Hot roadster of Miltonborough Zone 9. Circuit cruiser of the south.

He didn't notice the mess at first, he was too concerned that they should catch the London Orbital 11 exit for superdrive vehicles. It was easy to miss and Speed Marshals gave you on-the-spot debit points for travelling the normal routes in mode. There were tales of people never being able to get off the orbital route. There might also be Security Retrievers from the Malls. Too many kids had tried to leave the new Townships recently.

Absent WithOut Leave, as they called it.

You just had to be careful: miss the exit and you could find yourself out towards the west, in Hampstead Heath District 4 with the glow-worms! Most of the contaminates from 'the Great Mistake' hung out there.

The words 'London Orbital 11 EXIT 8' flashed a bright tangerine across the evening sky. Below this a deep red throbbed in front of a crack of yellow cloud cover: SUPERDRIVE AND JETDRIVE ONLY. He squinted. Hologram road signs were great except just after dusk. Then you couldn't be sure whether you were reading the setting

132

sun or tourist projection codes. It was a regular excuse among runaways for being in the wrong place and Speed Marshals had heard it loads of times.

'Certainly sir and what did the twilight tell you? Docklands Village Exit 7 in eight minutes? Can I see your licence tattoo please?'

The car entered 9 Minute Mode, locked for the next Exit Lane on Orbital 11 route.

No turning back now and take-away was every-where.

This was serious. Speedy was very car proud.

Sweet 'n' sour pork lay in the music centre drawer. Chicken breadcrumbs and fried rice lay in his lap. The combination platter of pork and beef ribs was all over the place.

The toys were ruined.

With a decisive manoeuvre of the auto-mode rectifier the car squealed into emergency climbdown. With a touch that could belong only to an accomplished Master of the Cortina X1-11 system, Speedy brought the car to a sudden halt.

Cars of all shapes and sizes roared past him, many searching for a way off the freeway. Some of the Factor 8 autos could hardly be seen at all, they were travelling so fast.

He sighed, counted to ten and thumped the car seat next to him.

'G-force! Damn G-force! The car is a mess!'

The Satellite Radio was playing Goldie Oldie Hour with Frambo Boyzer, the wildest DJ bounced down from space station 7, serving London Orbital, twenty-four hours; sound you could reach out and touch.

It was back to the year 1998 and an old Cliff Richard record.

The spot lighting of the freeway interchange flashed across the windscreen at regular intervals like sparkling bursts of fire cracker.

Speedy reached down into the firearms compartment and felt around for his spray of car deodoriser, but it wasn't there. The smell of take-away made him queasy. It was OK under his nose, just great down his throat, but no good at all when it was all over the car.

His car was his life, his amusement arcade on wheels. The Playpen: famous from Romford to Brighton 9 Contentment City, from Greenwich 7 to Oxford sector 4.

Great spec: twin vertical, custom lighting (not neon – but still flashy), parallel striping down the sides. Mirror chrome with platinum side rails on the headlights. Studded fender to spec 0.9.

The seat covers really began to smell now. Reconstituted road food didn't last long.

The humid summer day was cooling, and he needed to get out of his clothes and get the covers off the seats, before it got too dark. He needed a freeway Mall. He hated the Playpen to be in disarray.

Up ahead a hologram flashed an Exit number. It was unfamiliar but he decided to take it. His right hand tapped the car keyboard. The program slipped into his car RAM. The Playpen glided away, on to the Exit lane.

Speedy bit his lip. Hypnotised by route lights and private thoughts, he had forgotten the road.

He stared through the windscreen.

It was odd. Maybe it was the light or his mood. The exit seemed to be unnaturally quiet, even spooky. This stretch was not up to Orbital 11-90 standard.

He went cold. He had travelled this route before. This was nuke country, primitive territory, outland stuff. He half expected to come across a radioactive shoppers' sector. Even the four lanes of the Direction Sensor had cut back to two. He clicked down his window. The sulphur-like burn from the re-cycle units wafted into the car, hitting the take-away head on. Outside, 'China Syndrome' fireflies danced along the headlight path, glitter dust trees bowed, their knotted branches almost scraping the sides of the road.

He *was* off route. He mustn't panic.

Speedy wondered how he had got on to the Nuker District 4 route. You had to be very careful of *those* sectors. In any case this was not a road for a Cortina. This was a road for Hover Convoys, Spade Racers or other Roadies. Not a Cortina X1-11, and not *this* X1-11. He'd have to exit, it could ruin the gloss on his wheel trims.

Suddenly the 'Out of Sensor' warning light lit up on the dashboard. The transfer mode began to purr, automatically selected. The dashboard advised standard procedure:

MANUAL FORMAT MUST BE ENGAGED IN 5 SECONDS!

'Piss it!' he yelled, 'I've never had to do this on any Orbital freeway before.'

The road had reduced to little more than dirt and sand by now, the feel of the tyres told him so. He would have to do some real driving. He'd got out into the overgrowth. It could be dangerous, strange vegetation, strange everything.

There was nothing to see except the occasional red glow of eyes from the cloak of dark green. Mutants probably. He didn't want to think about it.

Suddenly, up ahead, a curious rainbow of colour blinked into the dusky sky.

It was not a hologram.

Speedy's eyes widened as the car got nearer. He could not believe it, here they were off the Orbital – a whole string of them. Real neon, old-style, tubed, flashy, but neat. Neon tubing pumping and buzzing out signs just like in the old days in the Piccadilly Circus viddy. Any custom car bodger in Miltonborough would give an arm and a leg and a year's vitamin ration for just four feet of pure neon.

A strip on the bumper and another across the boot would just complete the Cortina X1-11 to perfection, Speedy mused. It would be adding *the* final piece of jewellery. With proper battery back-up neon lit your car and made it an automobile for the gods.

The signs flashed out:

FUEL—RE-CYCLED AND REGULAR—YOUR CHOICE.

Lights chased dark spaces around the words.

Beyond this was a poorly lit side lot, like a car park.

Some old shack and a couple of pumps belonging to a place that had neon! He couldn't believe it.

The pumps were the old type and there they sat, right beside a re-cycle access point. Speedy made a turn without signalling and pulled on to the gravel driveway.

The illegal drive panted and wheezed its way through to shut-down. A whisper of black smoke squeezed out from under the chassis.

The Playpen stopped.

The fuel pumps stood like lonely sentries behind a long low wooden bar.

Speedy was intrigued. The pumps belonged in the Township Museum, they were so old. Perhaps this was a memorabilia stopping point, a Souvenir Centre, a clever gimmick to get people to stop for fuel. But who would stop here, anyhow?

People on Township exchanges, runaways like himself, perhaps.

The tumbledown shack waited in the shadows.

Somewhere out in the overgrowth giant glow toads croaked a chorus. The smell of radio ozone was stronger here. Rambling ivy was everywhere, dripping and winding its way from the branches of trees, holding everything firmly in its place. London's natural orbital.

There was a buzz in the air. Water gnats and other strange insects hurried busily from place to place. It was getting late and nature's nerves seemed on edge.

137

The central rough planked door of the shack was tightly shut. Two misty windows stared blankly on to the driveway from either side. An occasional shadow moved inside along with the sound of laboured movement.

Speedy watched the window. The curtain moved. Had somebody looked out at him?

There was a sudden crackle and then the fizz. He knew the sound.

In seconds the lot became a blend of colour and light. Neon sang with the night.

The dark greens and greys of the foliage over-lapped with a mix of blues, reds and oranges. The kaleidoscope of light projected upwards, etching the outline of the shack.

Speedy's nose twitched.

The smell of take-away returned.

He came back to earth with a bump. He was still covered in sauce.

The door of the shack swung open. The shape which shambled into the shadows was old and slow, catching its breath in short, sharp gasps. A thin spindle-like arm reached out to the handrail.

'Hello there!' said a voice.

Speedy felt better. The greeting was reassuring.

'D'you want fuel? Special this week, re-cycle or regular, choice is yours, I have both!'

It was difficult to make out the detail of the man's face. Speedy could only see an eye. The voice was strange, accented.

'Re-cycle, just to level 3.'

The man sucked his teeth, or something like teeth.

138

'I take exchanges, credit discs or cash if you've got it. Let me do this. There's some real Coca-Cola back there, not the reconstituted stuff, and I've got great bargains at my miniature shopping Mall. Go take a look. The coke's free.'

Speedy nodded and looked around for the 'Mall'. What a joke, a 'Mall' – out here!

The old man wheezed as he took the pump gun from its holder.

With slight hesitation, natural suspicion, Speedy crept around the back. The sounds of popping neon emptied into the evening air. There was no Mall, just a long wooden porch belonging to a onetime garage.

Laid out end to end in a semi-circle were lines of neon strips. Metallic foil had been fixed behind them so that light was directed upwards.

Blackboards shone in the glare of small floodlights, listing special offers in barely decipherable scrawl.

It was amazing. The prices were cheap, too cheap.

Behind the blackboards, on the walkway of the porch itself, lay a parade of metal buckets and wire baskets. Wire hooks in the roof supported tyres or inner tubes or fan belts for – Speedy held his breath – turbo neo-mods!

Speedy did a double take, his heart thumping. Now he realised. The man was an ex-Yank! One of the leftovers from the old Air Bases. This was a custom car bodger's paradise, a toy shop for motorway rodders, a heaven for road spinners.

It was a car accessory shopping mart. And better

stuff than the Mall! Special stuff. Hard-to-get stuff.
Illegal stuff!

The display was crude, but the goods were there!
Speedy could feel the saliva pooling inside his mouth.
His eyes turned to greedy drowning pools that would
gobble up every special offer if they could. He
glowed just thinking about the gadgets. Caution
gone, he stepped up to the porch for a better look.

In a small aluminium bucket to his left were
generation 5 feedback oscillators. These would fix
the kick-back problem without any trouble at all.
The Speed Marshals would never know that the
drive was a custom job. A split wooden stick held
a ragged-edged piece of card. The price was just
ridiculous – two tokens each or an exchange of
vitamins.

A steel hook above Speedy carried a '1 token
each' card and a string of silicon flow timing chains.
A quick inspection revealed that the links were
metallurgy 9 quality – these beauties would just
run and run.

The old man couldn't know the value of what
he carried.

Speedy's head span. You couldn't even get this
stuff on the Black Mall-Mart!

For the first time he noticed that there were
other rooms beyond the porch, but they were unlit
and blinds concealed what was inside.

A voice spoke up from behind him.

'Anything else you'd like? I've filled it up
with re-cycle. That's a great car you've got there.
Souped-up Ford?'

Speedy turned. The old man stood behind the glare of the neons. It was still difficult to see him properly, since the light reduced his outline to a fluorescent-edged shadow.

Was he glowing? He stood perfectly still, like a formal attendant awaiting orders.

'Just admiring your gear here. Where'd you get it all?'

There was a wheezy laugh. 'Why, a mixture mainly. I used to be around the old Air Bases. Some of it's from there but mostly it's reject gear, seconds, from those big Mall Chains.'

Then the old man stepped in front of the neons.

Speedy held his breath.

The old man was transformed.

The effect was dramatic. At first Speedy thought it must be a trick of the light. It wasn't just the fact that the old man was obviously a Contaminate. The tangled shock of light blue curly hair was disconcerting enough, but the unseeing ivory blank of an eye sent a shiver down Speedy's spine. There were other deformities too. The man was a Nuker.

The old man grinned.

These people were to be avoided. Victims of the 'Great Mistake', they had their own self-help districts. He should be back in his own sector! There was talk of a return to dark and ancient ways. The man shouldn't be trading, the business was illegal, but he probably knew that Marshals would never come out here. Too risky, and they were too careful ever to take risks.

The old man shifted forwards, an arm reaching out to the porch rail.

Suddenly Speedy understood the reason for the low-key lighting, the occasional handrails and the old man's slow shift and fumble. He'd already complimented Speedy on the Playpen, and he seemed to handle the pump OK so he couldn't be *completely* blind, but the odds were that he couldn't see that well.

Nukers gave Speedy the creeps.

Speedy had been wondering how to get his hands on all this equipment, how he could strike some deal. It was going to be easier than he thought. After all, the man was nearly blind, and he was an illegal Nuker! He wouldn't dare report trouble.

Speedy experimented, he waved his hands in front of the old man's face. He pointed. There was no response.

Blind as a fall-out sparrow.

'I'm interested in all the accessories, there're some great things.'

The old man laughed. The laugh was beginning to irritate Speedy.

'I suppose a lot of this interests a boy like you? You just look around, enjoy yourself, there's plenty for everybody. Cheaper than them Malls too. It won't disappear.'

'Old fool,' thought Speedy. 'That's where you're wrong. Someone was bound to happen by one day and snap it all up, and I think it might just be me.'

Speedy grew confident. He remembered the inner

142

rooms. He stepped up to the porch and gazed past the assorted buckets.

'That your stockroom back there?' he asked.

'Yes, sir.'

The question had pulled the old man up sharp and the laughter had stopped.

'Will you let me look? There could be something I'd want.'

The old man stood quite still.

'It's all on the porch. There's only special items there. Not ready for sale yet.'

Speedy said nothing.

A breeze suddenly blew by, ruffling the old man's strange blue curls.

A grin stretched out on Speedy's face.

'OK, that's fine, I'll carry on looking.'

The old man relaxed and turned back to the shack.

Speedy whispered beneath his breath.

'What trust. He's asking to be taken.'

The blue head turned a fraction. 'This was the kid all right,' the old man thought, 'the runaway from Miltonborough, as reported on the Home Viddy. A real accessory freak.'

From within the single ivory eye he saw.

Speedy played with the items which had been thrown together in the buckets, wishing he had a trailer so that he could dump the entire load into the back and take off.

Very gradually he eased his way to the rear of the porch, picking up a spare thrust-pack card from one of the buckets, pretending to pay it close attention.

143

In between counting the alpha chips he peered in through the porch window. A wedge of light from an open door stretched across the floor picking up the corners of old boxes.

Speedy could not believe his luck, the room was unlocked. The old man deserved to be robbed blind. Speedy sniggered. His mind was made up. He crept along the side of the shack, opened the door wider and slipped inside.

The light was poor but a quick forage amongst various boxes revealed the same kind of stuff that was on sale on the porch. Then Speedy saw something else.

A cardboard carton appeared to shift in front of his feet. He'd nearly tripped over it. He blinked hard. Was he seeing things? Had this toppled over from somewhere? Boxes didn't walk, he must have kicked it accidentally. He took a closer look.

He could just about read the scrawl on the side: 'Rejects. Tomorrow Stores. Security issue.' He peeled back the flaps and rummaged around inside. There were no hard edges, no circuit boards or pieces of engineering which would catch on his fingers. There was only softness.

It was comforting, a furry yielding which seemed to caress his fingers, to stroke his hand, circle his wrist and then . . . to envelop his arm. He pulled his hand away. What was in there?

He kicked the box back towards the doorway. Edges of a hairy fabric were highlighted by the glare of light.

Speedy sighed with relief. He'd thought it was

an animal. He pulled at the fabric. Several pieces of shaped fur tumbled out on to the floor.

This was unbelievable. Car-seat covers, they were car-seat covers just like in the old days at Motor Marts!

He continued sorting through the box. Matching furry pillows, dice, head-rest, accelerator cover. Even jacket. No, there were trousers too, an entire suit. A designer set! He had to have it – he'd never felt fabric so soft. This could set him up as king of the freeway, the ultimate custom.

'Sir, you've no business being here.'

Speedy dropped the jacket.

Silhouetted in the doorway was the old man, the backdrop of light somehow making him stronger. He looked less frail.

'I need car-seat covers. These.'

The old man shook his head.

'Not for sale. Most of this stock is special.'

'Not for sale?'

'I'm sorry, this isn't for you. You see those things need checking. This is really special stuff. You've got to be an ace to handle some of those items. You need experience, you haven't got it. Some of the accessories were Security Issue for the Mall guards. The seat covers, for example, well, they really are unique.'

The old man grinned inwardly.

'Make him want them real bad,' he thought.

Speedy began to boil.

'So? Come on!'

The old man laughed.

'You're a Township boy aren't you, bet you're AWOL as we used to say at the base. Why don't you go on home, there'll be Retriever Guards out here soon!'

This Nuker Contaminate was stupider than Speedy had thought.

Speedy's anger displaced any nagging doubts about what he was going to do. What he HAD to do. He got to his feet. He certainly wasn't going home.

Speedy felt cooler than the sub-mode air conditioner he'd recently installed. The Playpen just glided along, nice and easy. The sensor-driven auto-route and the softness of the new seat covers made driving like riding a cloud. The boot was packed with neon and as many of the other accessories as he could cram in. A few boxes sat on the back seat and other items lay below the dashboard.

The smell of take-away was still there, he'd had to hurry away and most of the spilt food was still lodged under the mats. But he *had* to slip the new covers on and he *had* to change into the suit.

He felt like a freeway king.

The fur of his new suit melted into the classy new covers. Matching.

He engaged manual mode more frequently than he would have done normally, just so that he could feel the softness of the accelerator cover. He had taken his shoes off as soon as he sat in the seat. Whatever the fabric was, the feel of the pedal cover was extraordinary.

He stroked the accelerator with the bare ball

of his foot. Soft as a girl's hair. Smooth as skin.

The engine purred in response. Speedy's nerve ends tingled. This was the ultimate in sensual driving.

The night was cooling, and he felt good. He felt guiltless. It had been so easy, especially with all that pompous crap the old man had spewed up. It had made him glad to do it.

Speedy's right arm reached down to see what else there might be in the box of tricks. He'd noticed a few old CD ROM Discs – there might even be some good music there. He felt around at the bottom of the box. Then his hand touched something wet and sticky.

'Hell!'

He lifted his fingers from the goo. The barbecue had seeped through the bottom of the box. He wiped his hand on the furry mat. He had no choice, car proud or not.

Something like a cat's tongue scraped the back of his fingers.

The soft fur of the covers brushed the sauce off with ease. It almost licked it off.

Speedy frowned. That had felt odd. He needed some music, the late hour was causing him to imagine things.

He grabbed a CD ROM disc, dropped it into the mouth of the dash-player. It was a real oldie, but in quad-dimensional sound.

This was driving.

Speedy rapped out an accompanying rhythm on the central module generator, breaking into double

147

time when the drum beat came through the front speakers.

Strange.

He knew this oldie well but the percussion was much louder in this version. It must be the acoustics – the effect of furry seat covers.

Then he realised that the front speakers were playing something very different from the ones at the rear. At times they crossed and complemented one another, then they would hit head on.

There was a distinct humming, and it wasn't on the disc. A light shone up into Speedy's face. Could the inside of the car be glowing?

Speedy's right hand dropped to the control bar and ejected the disc.

The music sttopped, but there was another noise. Speedy paid careful attention. He'd heard this once before.

His blood turned to milk. It was isotope interference.

He snapped off the central control dip-switch. It made no difference. The car had its own source of power now.

The music centre glowed, fluorescent.

He heard it, loudly and clearrly. It was disgusting. An enormous thunderous belch.

A huge sickening bubble of stale air wafted up under his nose. That was too real.

He glanced at the floor where the take-away barbecue had been.

His eyes grew wide, a cry stuck in his throat. Several large chunks of meat were slowly and systematically disappearing into the pile at the base of the seat cover. Each spare rib was carefully twisted and turned by a ripple of fur, as if it were being examined.

He caught his breath. The covers heaved like waves, glowing with a moon grey light.

Then it hit him, he knew what they must be doing. *But seat covers can't eat take-away!*

The cover at his back rippled downwards to the car floor. The softness pulsed.

Another belch rose from the floor, foul air filling the car.

The rippling movements became folds of seat cover, enveloping the remains of the barbecue. Juices flowed and swirled at his feet.

Beneath the humming he could hear a new sound. A harder sound, a crunching sound.

He cried out.

The sole of his right foot was only stroked at first. Then something small and wet, something which probed and slithered at the bottom of his foot like a searching tongue, darted in between his toes and sucked long and hard.

He was yanked down off the seat. He tried desperately to pull himself back up by the steering wheel. His eyes filled with tears as he was dragged down on to the accelerator pedal.

Then, pandemonium. The inside of the car rolled and lapped around him. Soft folds thrashed angrily as patches of furry wetness sucked and slithered. His suit seemed to be pulling at the seat covers.

Whatever it was it had liked the barbecue. Now it wanted something else.

Speedy managed to splutter a final pleading cry.

'No, please, please, no!'

As the car filled with digestive juices he saw gum-pink flesh yawn towards him. The radiation safety dial arrow on his dashboard was way over.

As he disappeared into the luxury of real fur, he yearned for the security of Miltonborough.

The covers let out a loud and final belch.

The Speed Marshal had noticed the X1-11 before. Marshal 232 had always had a secret yen to be able to pull the boy in one day. This one was a constant runner from the Township.

But he was asking for trouble out here.

As the dawn broke lazily across the London Orbital the Marshal could see that although there had been an accident, this was no write-off derelict.

The Ford Cortina lay silently beside the Exit crash barrier. The driver had probably fallen asleep at the wheel during manual mode. It happened all the time.

The Marshal peered inside.

The tinted windows made it difficult to see. The geiger on his belt started to crackle and twitch.

With a sten-gun pellet at the ready he opened the passenger door. The smell was awful. He stared in disbelief and incomprehension.

Why should a Cortina X1-11 be crammed full of fur?

He grabbed his handkerchief and put it to his

150

mouth. Something red and sticky and unpleasant dripped from the corner of the door.

His mouth dried. He feared the worst at first, then a scrap of cardboard fell out on to the ground. It had a familiar red and white design.

That made him feel better. It was just another abandoned car full of trash and left-over take-away food, but it was strange that there was a contamination reading. He would phone in and get the De-Nukers out.

He picked up the carton lid.

Suddenly he heard a rustle. A blue-uniformed guard with large drop shades rose up from the other side of the car.

On his lapel were the words: Security Retriever.

'It's OK, Officer. He's one of ours. A Township runner. We got him though. New method. Had my doubts I must say but it seems to have worked. We've started to use the Nukers and this one got this kid to take one of our "Rovers".'

The smile widened beneath the sightless eyes.

'More effective than the four-legged kind! Always thought that mutation must be good for something one day!'